Last Stop Havana
THE FIFTH RUSSIAN THRILLER

– STEPHEN B. MORRISEY –

An environmentally friendly book printed and bound in England by
www.printondemand-worldwide.com

Mixed Sources
Product group from well-managed
forests, and other controlled sources
www.fsc.org Cert no. TT-COC-002641
© 1996 Forest Stewardship Council
FSC

PEFC Certified
This product is
from sustainably
managed forests
and controlled
sources
www.pefc.org
PEFC
PEFC/16-33-415

This book is made entirely of chain-of-custody materials

www.fast-print.net/store.php

LAST STOP HAVANA: THE FIFTH RUSSIAN THRILLER
Copyright © Stephen B. Morrisey 2014

A catalogue record for this book is available from the British Library

ISBN 978-178456-108-6

First published 2014 by
FASTPRINT PUBLISHING
Peterborough, England.

For those who know the risks of adventure

One

WITH a practised flick of the barrel, the handgun was fully loaded. Water dropped from the inside roof of a damp road bridge at the side of the wide river. Through the bridge and across the river stood the Hotel Ukraina, one of the seven skyscrapers built by Stalin which for years had dominated the Moscow skyline. The buildings, tall, austere, a feat of Soviet architecture where size and square lines of hard granite were used to project power, still evoke memories of the glories of Russia'a Soviet past. Power through domination and discipline. The seven skyscrapers towered over the sprawling capital city and showed the outside world the Soviet Union's indomitable determination, no matter the miseries inside the buildings, the rampant mice and cowering citizens.

A boat was moored along the footpath at the side of the bridge. It was some thirty meters long and had two storeys. It was an old motor boat which had been converted into a floating casino by virtue of a roulette table, a couple of card tables, an improvised bar and a dozen cabins. The cabins were rented out for short periods for those who could not stumble home or for those who had other things on their mind after a heavy night gambling and drinking. Music was punctuated by peals of laughter.

It was a cold night. A man was standing under the bridge. He was poorly dressed in an old suit. A blacked-out BMW drew up ten meters from the bridge and a much more smartly dressed man got out. He wore a polo-necked jumper under an expensive black suit. In an exchange that barely took a couple of seconds the first man passed the second man a long paper tube and pocketed in return a thick envelope.

It was a quiet night on the casino boat. As Moscow started to close down in the early hours of a September morning, the players on the casino boat either drifted away or settled into the cabins until the late morning. The music stopped and the only sound from the boat which echoed under the bridge was that of a repetitive splash and thud as a lifeless body in an old suit bumped constantly against a porthole of one of the cabins on the casino boat.

Two

WITH a practised flexing of the fingers, the garrotte hummed. A doll made out of black cloth, strands of wool and small bent pieces of wicker dangled from the rear-view mirror of an old car. It had a large needle through where a heart would have been were the doll not so decrepit and falling apart. The car was an 1950's Buick and was parked on the headland of the Malecon, the broad esplanade which runs for five miles along the coast in Havana, the capital of Cuba.

The car was a short distance from the Hotel Nacional, the huge Art Deco-style building opened in 1930 at the height of Cuba's popularity for the rich and famous from America and the rest of the world. The hotel had been the party centre of the world where the famous and beautiful smoked, drank and danced the nights away as a hungry native population watched on and waited for their time to come. Underneath the hotel lies a labyrinth of hidden caves which were used to defend the city from raids in the centuries when Spain ruled the New World as well as becoming a haven for smugglers then and right up to the modern day.

As well as the driver of the car, who looked to be as old as car and who wore a cap pulled tightly down on his head, there was another man in the back seat of the car.

A man dressed in a khaki suit and carrying a steel briefcase approached the car. A back passenger door opened and without any words being exchanged the man got into the car which sped away leaving rising dust in its wake. It was a sultry evening.

"You know what we want," said the man in the man in the back.

"I have no idea what you are talking about," replied the man in the khaki suit in an English public school accent. "I was just told that a car would be outside and take me ba.. back to my hotel." He had begun to stutter. The sight of the man winding a thin piece of wire around his fingers had made his eyes almost pop out of their sockets.

"The payment has been made," continued the other man in a very calm fashion as he relieved the other man of the steel briefcase.

"I have no idea," replied the man, a tear forming in his eye. "I am a geologist. What do you ww.. want?"

An hour later a body in a khaki suit was bobbing up and down near an outcrop of rocks in the sea off the Malecon. His throat had been slit from side to side by the most precise means known to man.

Three

WITH a practised swish of the blade on the grinding stone, the hunting knife was sharpened. Activity at the quayside had subsided as the evening drew in. The heat of the day was slowly evaporating. The Freedom Tower stood proudly and dominated the downtown Miami skyline. A building whose tower was inspired by the Giralda bell tower of the Cathedral of Seville in Spain. It was used in the 1960's as the first port of call for the million or so refugees who fled from Cuba after Fidel Castro's Communist Revolution in 1959. The building held many tales of terror but stood as a beacon to those refugees who dreamt of one day reversing Castro's Revolution and imposition of Communism on the hitherto decadent, impoverished but fundamentally free island of Cuba.

A white van had been parked near the waterfront for several hours. A man approached the quayside on foot.

He was very agitated and his body movements could have been mistaken for a drug addict searching for a fix. He was holding a long, thin tube. Inside the van two men had been using banks of surveillance equipment. They gave the 'all clear' to a man in the front passenger seat who then got out of the van. The man took out a wallet and checked the badge inside. He walked over to the man on the quayside.

The man on the quayside stared at the man. "You're not Tony," he said his agitation visibly increasing.

"We are Tony's friends," replied the man holding his badge up in front of the man's face. "I am Agent Green."

"Tony said I would get political asylum and witness protection. That I can stop running."

"You sure can say that," said Agent Green taking the tube from the man. "You sure can say that."

Thirty minutes later a body was floating next to a small motor boat moored at the quayside under the darkening Miami skyline.

Four

MIAMI was hosting a business conference for geologists from all around the world. It did not sound very interesting in itself with topics such as 'The Geology of the Florencia Gold-Telluride Deposit' and 'Reducing the Risks of Extraction in Volcanic-Intrusive Strata'. However, the conference, which was held every two years, was for geologists who specialised in gold and, in particular, in the prospecting and extraction of new gold deposits. The conference was unique and attracted delegates from the four corners of the globe – from South America, Australasia, North America and the Far East of Russia and virtually every other gold-mining country in between.

The delegates were as diverse as their countries they came from and actual qualified geologists were a small minority of the delegates. Corporate executives, politicians, mining experts and seasoned treasure hunters filled the hotels – all looking to hear the slightest hushed rumour of a new discovery, all keen to understand new techniques for discovering deposits or extracting gold from complex geological structures and compositions. Hot spots at the moment were rumoured to be on the east coast of South America and in several locations in Cuba which lay just a hundred miles south of Miami across the Straits of Florida.

When the Spanish discovered Cuba and the New World in the fifteenth century Cuba turned out to be a huge disappointment as it only had small gold deposits of its own. The Spanish though soon afterwards discovered the amazing amounts of gold and silver mined by the Incas and Aztecs and for centuries gold and silver flowed from South America to Spain and then on to the rest of the world as Spain built its empire.

Cuba became the major staging post for the many ships that plied the routes to and from South America and it became rich from gold and silver shipped legally and, on occasions, illegally. It was also infamous for harbouring pirates and smugglers. It was widely believed that Cuba came to have more gold hidden in secret hoardes in the myriad of caves and underground caverns along its coastlines than actual gold in its gold deposits in the ground. Now though attention was focussing on several exisiting and new gold deposits in

Cuba and international interest was growing sharply. New extraction techniques were said to be the major factor.

The first day of the conference had several lectures and then two Q&A sessions. The formal dinner of the conference was set for the following evening and this evening there was an evening cruise on offer and many of the delegates had signed up for it as this was the informal night of the conference. This was the time for unseen business and quiet negotiations and also for partying – the networking glue of any international conference of value.

The Freedom of the Seas cruise ship had docked at the quayside and the day cruisers were disembarking before the ship was readied for the evening. The day cruise had been to an island in the Bahamas for snorkeling and a barbeque on a beach. A man and woman with two young children walked down the gangplank. The children were swinging on the rails whenever they had a chance. A large sign announcing the 'Miami Gold Conference Evening Cruise' caught the eye of the man and he stopped to study it.

The sign had a map of part of an island as its background. A map in the style of a seventeenth century hand-drawn parchment with a large ornate compass in the bottom left hand corner. In the top right hand corner was a logo of a pile of gold with a snake wrapped around it. The man raised an eyebrow. Jack Kelly, fresh off a day's cruise with his wife and twins in the middle of a Disney and Miami family holiday, was immediately plunged back into the harsh winter of Moscow. The memory was alluring. Piles and piles of pieces of gold – gold which at the time he had not been sure whether it was freshly-mined or had already been fashioned into ingots and coins, or 'doubloons' as they were better known in historical and treasure-hunting circles.

Five

FLOXLY, the British Prime Minister, had normalised relations with the US's President Stone after the debacle of the Aden disaster and the Uzbek gas privatisation. There was still a strong frost between Russia and America but Floxly was quite content to be out of the crossfire and to be on terms with both Stone and Russia's President Bunin. The American Ambassador in London was meeting with Floxly and the British Foreign Secretary, Douglas Cummings.

"For once," said the Ambassador, "I am happy to say that I am able to share some important new intelligence with you. Intelligence from the CIA as a sign of our re-established special relationship in security matters."

"President Stone and I did agree that we should level a lot more between us as our countries have always done so in the past," replied Floxly with a smile.

"To be fair to him he was under severe pressure for a while from our arms lobby but he has reasserted himself strongly," continued the Ambassador.

Floxly and Cummings nodded.

"The intelligence is that we are very hopeful of some positive developments in our own backyard," said the Ambassador.

"Central America?" asked Cummings.

"Near," replied the Ambassador with a practised smile. "In Cuba, in fact."

"Cuba!" exclaimed Floxly and Cummings in unison.

Cuba was one of the biggest sources of dispute between the Americans and the Former Soviet Union ever since Fidel Castro ousted the American-backed dictator, Batista, in 1959 through a Communist coup. Since independence from Spain in 1899 Cuba had effectively been controlled by the Americans for sixty years through several puppet dictators and the implementation of the Americans' so-called 'rights to intervene'. In the early 1960's as a direct result of Castro's coup almost a million people fled the new Cuban Communist regime principally to America.

Cuba then became one of the focal points of the Cold War between East and West. When the Soviets put nuclear rockets into Cuba for a short period in 1962 the world stood on the brink of nuclear war.

"Yes," continued the Ambassador warming to his theme, "events are favouring us finally after over fifty years. The Castro family grip is loosening every day and we do not believe Russian support to be anything like as strong as it was in Soviet times. And this is despite some recent attempts by Bunin to make up for the disastrous effect the stopping of Communist aid to Cuba had after the collapse of the Soviet Union."

Floxly was very surprised but he did not say anything.

"There is also a groundswell of support on the island which is getting bolder by the hour and great excitement is building in the so-called 'Exiles' based in Florida. After many years of complaining the Exiles have evolved into several core groups. They are now a credible poltical and lobbying force. The spread of mobile phones and the Internet on the island also means that the Cuban authorities can no longer block contact between people on the island and in America. In short given the right combination of these factors and," paused the Ambassador reverting to his more diplomatic tone, "some specific initiatives by certain groups, which, of course, I have no knowledge about, there is a growing confidence that the ruling clan cannot last out for very much longer and Cuba will return to a proper democracy. And when it does we are sure that it will once again soon become part of an extended America. The fifty-first state, even."

Floxly and Cummings had listened pretty much in silence. This was news. This was clearly the US initiating a play which although seemingly on a Caribbean island could easily escalate into a regional conflict or worse. Had the Americans forgotten their previous disastrous attempt to 'retake' Cuba when US groups landed at the infamous Bay of Pigs expecting to be welcomed by the Cuban people only to leave humiliated and in so doing massively exacerbate the Cold War? Was it a high risk attempt to see how Bunin would react? This was a geo-political risk like no other on the planet.

"And," concluded the Ambassador with a flourish his cheeks now flushed with the excitement which had flowed with his words, "it might be a sensible move to alert any of your assets or your people on the island. Just in case there are events which might not be controllable."

Cummings gave a grave look at Floxly as the Ambassador stood up and Floxly thanked him. Prior to the meeting he had just been informed of the discovery of the body of a senior British geologist on the island. It had looked at first like some form of ritual killing but the theft of the geologist's briefcase at a critical phase of his work meant that a more basic motive was now suspected.

Six

FLOXLY called Russia's President Bunin within seconds of the American Ambassador leaving. The two world leaders enjoyed the telephone calls between them. They spoke very calmly even when one of them faced a crisis. The calls had worked very effectively in the past to pass on gentle warnings or simply to exchange important information.

"I hope you have fully recovered, Vladimir, after the incident on the way to Wimbledon," said Floxly. On Bunin's drive into Wimbledon several months earlier two gunmen had tried to assassinate Bunin but both of them had been stopped at the last moment.

"Oh, yes, David. A summer split between the White Nights of St Petersburg and the tropical climate of Sochi is the best holiday anyone in the world could have. Why all of Northern Europe invades Spain, France and Italy in the summer has always been a mystery to me!"

Bunin did indeed sound fully recovered to Floxly and some.

"Weather and wine, Vladimir, and cheap wine at that, tend to be the attractions," replied Floxly who himself had been a pretty typical Brit abroad with a week on Mallorca and a long weekend in Tuscany in the summer. "I have just had a strange visit from the American Ambassador in London which I thought I should tell you about," continued Floxly reverting to the reason for the call whilst still pondering whether if he reduced UK taxes on wine and spirits then a lot more Brits would holiday in the UK. The UK weather killed that thought.

"Yes, my line of communication with President Stone is still to be reconnected," replied Bunin.

"I understand fully. The reason for the visit being strange was that he was trying to warn me about Cuba."

"Cuba!" exclaimed Bunin becoming animated. "Our land of sugar and cigars!"

"Yes," continued Floxly enjoying knowing something which Bunin did not. "Seems like the Americans want to take it back once and for all. Seems the Americans think that the break in your relations with Cuba after the fall of the Soviet Union has still to be fully recovered."

Bunin laughed and then after a pause said, "hands off, please. We have been working hard to re-establish our comradely relations with our Cuban cousins recently. We have even started some military cooperation projects. They are becoming an asset to us once again and the Americans will have no joy there."

"Somehow I did not think you would give up on Cuba so easily," replied Floxly.

"Thank you for the information, David."

And with that the call ended with Bunin's laughter echoing down the phone line.

Floxly made another quick call. He knew that Kelly had gone on a holiday with his family and that they were not a million miles away from Cuba. Perhaps an extension to his holiday might appeal to him.

Seven

RUSSIA'S President Bunin's private office in the Kremlin was sparsely furnished compared to the general opulence of his official State office a few doors away. His private office had a desk with a chair behind and three chairs in front arranged in a fan arrangement. There were two large maps on two of the walls and a four-sided chessboard which he used to play against imaginary foes or terrorist groups simultaneously. His main preoccupation was never a one-on-one situation but the knock-on effects any moves in a specific situation or conflict had on other groups or on the surrounding countries such was the interlocking nature of his empire and those who opposed him.

Bunin was with Igor Zelinsky, the Head of the FSB. Zelinsky had once been Bunin's boss when they were both in the KGB and Bunin had made him head of the

FSB, the successor to the KGB, as soon as he had become President.

"You said that Floxly had called you, Vladimir," said Zelinsky.

"Yes," replied Bunin, "he confirmed what we already knew about America's latest big project."

"That they want Cuba back?" said Zelinsky. Zelinsky had a soft spot for the exotic Caribbean island having spent a short spell of his career there when the old Cold War was at its height. A time when close bonds were formed between KGB agents and operatives in other friendly agencies throughout South and Central America. "So shall we accelerate our plans?"

"We should prioritise them certainly and especially increase as much pressure as we can on our allies to be ready for the Americans. We must increase the military cooperation exercises with the Cubans as soon as possible. There are certain valuable reserves on the island which are also attractive," added Bunin who particularly liked to combine any economic gains with political advancements whenever possible.

"The gold reserves we know are still low by international comparisons," said Zelinsky who remembered how false rumours of vast gold finds on Cuba had been such a feature in the heyday of the

Soviet-Cuban entente. Rumours engineered by the Cubans to encourage largesse by Moscow in providing soft loans to prop up the Castro socio-economic dreams.

Bunin smiled at Zelinsky. "It is the nickel we are focussing on, Igor. And who do we have in Cuba?"

"Several teams but the lead agents are under cover as executives of Cyprus Gold Limited. Their primary task is to acquire the nickel mining rights you have identified which are mixed in with the gold deposits. And maybe a little gold on the side."

A brief frown flickered across Bunin's face – Nazarov and Varonsky. Long-time KGB stalwarts in South and Central America but both of whose careers had stalled in the FSB. "Are they loyal, Igor?"

"Let's just say that they were with me in Cuba and that I have a certain hold over them. They like to think of themselves as a little autonomous as so many of our agents out in the field do these days."

"Well, I trust you will be able to control them," said Bunin with a smile at his long-trusted colleague, "and make sure they keep their moonlighting work to a minimum. And what of Anna?" asked Bunin with a barely detectable touch of haste in his voice. He had realised immediately that with Nazarov and Varonsky he now definitely needed an extra pair of eyes and ears on the ground. Cuba was some six thousand miles away and on the other side of the world from Moscow and he needed to be able to watch and to act in real time.

"Several days ago she assumed her responsibilities as the new press officer for Cyprus Gold and she has already joined the team in Cuba," said Zelinsky.

Eight

THE delegates had finally taken their seats for the second day of the Miami Gold Conference. Copious amounts of black coffee and bottled water were being drunk by many of the delegates. The previous evening's cruise had been a great success. The morning session would see plenty of struggles with yawns, drooping eyelids and the occasional snore.

The nationalities of some of the delegates stood out and as delegates from specific companies tended to sit together this made some of the nationalities stand out even more. The Australians were the most casually dressed and smuggled in cans of beer in their conference bags. The Arabs were traditionally dressed in their white thwabs. The Africans stood out with the most with brightly-coloured shirts while the Cubans were noticeable for the generally poor quality of their clothing.

It was more difficult to divide up the Americans and Europeans. Another way of telling who was from where were the name badges which had names and companies on them, although companies from a specific country might not actually be from that country if the company was legally registered elsewhere. This was true for three companies in particular.

Cyprus Gold Limited had a delegation of three. The two men wore floral shirts, dark sunglasses and they were heavily sunburnt. They did not have the olive-like complexion of natives from the Mediterranean rather the flatter faces and pale skin more indicative of Slavic people. The third delegate, a young woman, was pure Russian. Long strikingly blond hair fell down around her shoulders and a stern attractiveness emanated from her face.

Newgold N.V. of the Netherland Antilles also had three delegates. Two of the men looked as though they worked in the City of London with their Saville Row suits and highly polished black shoes although they had discarded their silk ties in the heat. The third man who was quietly taking a call on his mobile again looked to be British. He had a bushy beard and was wearing a green cardigan with leather patches on the elbows so stereotypical of a casually-dressed British Foreign Office diplomat. The company was in essence British. Its country of registration was purely for tax avoidance.

The third company, the Canadian-Cuban Mining Corporation (Bermuda Ltd) or CCMC for short, although formally registed in Bermuda was ostentatiously Canadian and proud of it. The Canadian flag with its red maple leaf on a white and red striped background was plastered over everything its two delegates had – name badges, briefcases, notebooks and pens. The giveaway would only be picked up by a North American linguistic expert. One man was undoubtedly from Quebec in eastern Canada, the other though occasionally let slip the vowels of a native of Fairfax County, Virginia.

As the lunch break neared the British diplomat received a message on his mobile phone. He quietly excused himself and left without creating much disruption. He should have stayed. Outside of the conference centre he walked briskly to a parking lot and entered the stairwell. As he came up the concrete stairs two men pounced and dragged him out of the stairwell and into a corner of the parking lot. There were only a handful of cars parked on this level of the parking lot. One man held him tightly from behind, the other pressed the tip of a large knife to his throat.

"Man," said the man with the knife, "you are way beyond your limit, Gifford." He was dark-skinned with a flat face, almost Amazonian, and he spoke with a Caribbean rasp.

Gifford, which was the man's first name, had stopped struggling. His legs had turned to jelly and he was breathing heavily.

"Thought you could escape your debts, did you," continued the man as a sliver of blood oozed onto the tip of the knife.

"No, no," replied Gifford rapidly. His breathing was getting worse.

"As soon as you are back on the island we want the cash or your wife's jewellery and if you don't come back to the island we will hunt you down where ever you run to." As the man finished he drew the knife across Gifford's throat with an evil smile.

Gifford did not doubt him.

"That's why we came here. Just to remind you and give you a taste of what will happen and to show you what you will look like if you mess with us."

Gifford's eyes widended in pure horror as the man unwrapped a red silk cloth and took out a gruesome-looking doll. It had a beard and a cardigan and Gifford stared at the grotesque image of himself. The doll had a rope around its neck. The man let the doll dangle from the rope. Then as the man behind tightened his grip on Gifford, there was a loud clanking sound from the other end of the parking lot. Both men froze and then with a brief glance at each other they ran off to the stairwell. The doll was hastily wrapped back up in the red silk cloth as they ran.

Gifford sank to his knees as a camera took a series of photographs of the backs of the men and of Gifford. A young woman with long blond hair then put the camera in her handbag. She had not needed to take out her handgun.

Nine

THE Ministry for Energy and Mines in Havana occupies a four-storey neoclassical-style building on Avenida Salavador Allende, a major road which runs through the Centro Habana district to the Vedado district of the city. It has eight tall, slender columns in front of two flights of stone steps at its entrance. People were mingling and many smoking on the steps before entering. Security checks were perfunctory.

The conference room for the meeting was decorated with two large fresco-style paintings on its walls. The first depicted a series of mythical creatures including mermaids, fairies and goblins who were surrounded by geometrical symbols of triangles, star-shaped pentagrams and spirals. The impression was of the basic elements of the earth and the spirits who inhabit the sea, rivers and fields. The second painting was more poignant. It showed mines full of workers bent double in their labours and straining to pull carts full of minerals out of the mines. It also showed fields of sugar cane and again workers sweating and gritting their teeth as they swung machetes to harvest the sugar canes. The images evoked slavery and Colonial times. The two paintings contrasted the innate beauty and mysticism of the earth with the oppression of its people. It was Cuba's past.

The Minister who strode up to a letern on a podium infront of the paintings was, however, thoroughly modern looking. He was dressed as an archetypal businessman from Madrid. Exquisite hand-made light blue suit, yellow shirt and sparkling gold-striped silk tie. His black shoes shone from a deep polishing and his silver designer spectacles gave him the cool air of control. He annouced himself as Xavier de la Rosa, El Ministre del Ministerio de Energía y Minas, and after a few more words of greeting in Spanish he switched to English. He was accompanied on the podium by three other men seated behind a table.

"Senoras y Senores, Ladies and Gentlemen, it gives me great pleasure to see so many of you here today. For me, my ministry and my governemnt it is proof that the international community is once again commited to investment in our country. We have experienced good and bad times over the last fifty years with our international partners and we still face the huge challenges which the US embargo on trade with us creates."

The minister paused to see if there was any reaction to his reference to the US embargo but none came. He was addressing business people with a clear interest in mining and mining for gold. He hoped that politics would be off the agenda as far as they were concerned.

"We are modernising our country at an increasing pace and we are fortunate that advances in mining technologies means that the long-rumoured riches of our gold deposits will soon become a reality with your help and investments."

The minister paused again to look at his audience who were all listening to him carefully. He had spent a short time at the recent Miami Gold Mining Conference and been introduced to most of the main mining companies represented in the room. He then went on to explain that his ministry would shortly auction six concessions to mine for gold in partnership with the Cuban governement. The concessions were a combination of several old deposits and some newly-discovered ones. They were concentrated in three different parts of Cuba. In the Holgin province in the east were the deposits called San Andres, Punta Garda and Pedro Soto. In the Pinas del Rio province in the west were Santa Lucia and Dora Franciso. And finally in the south eastern tip of the island in Santiago de Cuba was Dos Palmas.

A maximum of two concessions per bidder would be allowed and in order to run an effective auction all companies who wanted to bid would need to qualify for the approved shortlist. Application forms for the shortlist would be available after this announcement and could be submitted as soon as possible thereafter. The shortlist would be announced within fourteen days.

As he finished speaking there was a general hum of approval from all present. Three well-dressed young woman then moved into the audience and distributed folders with the application forms in to anyone who signaled they wished to take one. At the same time a woman dressed in a violet silk cowl, a type of tunic with a hood, entered the conference room as well. She held a two-foot long metal rod with feathers tied to one end. The minister was about to ask if there were any questions about the forms but he paused and looked at the woman. The woman mumbled quickly under her breath and pointed the rod at the painting on the wall depicting the workers in the mines. She then left. The room had gone quiet. After a few seconds questions started to be asked. The minister held up his hand.

"Ladies and gentlemen, I fear the lady came into the room by mistake. There are other conferences on today and she obviously mistook us for the Tourist Board." A peel of gentle laughter crossed the room and the minister continued. "Now any questions about the process and the forms?"

The press conference was soon wrapped up and the strange appearance by the woman forgotten. Forgotten by most. The minister for one though would not forget. He had quickly and effectively made light of the incident but he had recognised the language and the meaning. The woman had invoked Oggun, the voodoo god of iron and minerals, and asked him to destory anyone who removed minerals from the sacred lands of Cuba. Cuba's past was not quite finished yet. The modernising minister might well have his work cut out to revive the Cuban gold mining industry but it might not be foreign investors who would be the hardest to deal with.

Ten

THE call to Kelly had a familiar ring to it. The Kelly
family was leaving the hotel to take the shuttle bus to
the airport for the flight home at the end of their holiday.
Kelly felt immediately as if Floxly must have been
watching him on a CCTV or by some other device.

"Jack," said Floxly, "heading home I presume?"

"Yes, Prime Minister," replied Kelly already sensing
that a request was seconds away. "Our flight is in three
hours."

"Well, Jack," continued Floxly hesitating, "I am afraid
that I have another favour to ask."

"It is not to do with a treasure hunt, gold possibly?"
joked Kelly. The logo on the conference sign came back
to him. He had seen something very similar to it before.
It had been one of those unqiue events in the
tumultuous times of the New Russia coming out of

Communism in the mid-1990's. It was an exhibition in the Kempinski Hotel in Moscow of long-forgotten maps and coins which Peter the Great had ammassed on his voyage of discovery to Europe in 1697, his so-called Grand Embassy - his very succesfull attempt to take European knowledge and skills back to his new capital of St Petersburg.

On his visit to Amsterdam to study shipbuilding Peter the Great and his entourage and befriended a Dutch explorer of the New World of South America and Peter the Great had returned with an arrany of maps and coins from that era predominantly of Spanish origin. These items had subsequently been stored in the vaults of the Hermitage Museum in St Petersburg where they had lain ever since. Kelly remembered that one map was rumoured to be one of several copies which the Dutch explorer had surrepticiously had made of an original map of so-called hidden gold. The copies had been done by memory from a fleeting study of the original which had been spirited away to a powerful and rich family's castle back in Spain. The copies were not perfect copies.

With the opening up of Russia in the mid-1990's some of the long-disregarded items from Peter the Great's Grand Embassy had been uncovered and a deal struck with the Spanish Embassy and a private Spanish company to sponsor an exhibition of the unique items first in the Hermitage itself and then in Moscow. Kelly had had meetings he remembered with the Spanish company about potential investments in a massive Russian sugar beet collective. Before Kelly could think any further Floxly was continuing the call.

"As always, Jack, you seem to be two steps ahead," replied Floxly with genuine warmth in his laugh. "Yes, there might be gold involved. A couple of days ago one of our UK companies lost its most senior geologist in strange circumstances."

"Oh?" said Kelly.

"Yes, the geologist has been found dead and it was in Cuba. He was working for Newgold, a British company registered in the Netherland Antilles. And I fear now that Cuba might become a bit of a battleground. We need someone to assist our Consul in Havana. Someone not obviously from the Foreign Office in London so-to-speak. Someone who can operate there without getting our Ambassador involved," Floxly paused. Since his conversations with the Americans and Bunin, he and Cummings had convinced themselevs that Cuba could very well become an international powder keg in the very near future and they had decided that they would have to alert Kelly to the possibility. "And Jack, there may well be some involvement from the Americans and possibly the Russians in Cuba very shortly. There might be a bit of a collision," he added. "Do you think you can help?"

Later that night as Kelly's wife and two children were fast asleep on their flight home, Kelly stepped off a plane in the Jose Marti airport in Havana. He had flown from Miami via Grand Cayman as flights from the United States into Cuba were still not allowed. The air was surprisingly cooler than in Miami. As he approacehd the exit an old painting above the door caught his eye. It was a depiction of a religious figure with a staff-like rod and a dog walking up a hillside with sheep in the background. It looked like Saint Peter, the Apostle, who was often shown as a shepherd. Kelly stopped for a moment and read the name under the picture. It was not Saint Peter but Papa Legba, the voodoo god who acts as the go-between between humans and the voodoo gods known as 'loas'.

Kelly frowned and then smiled to himself as he remembered one of the priests who taught him at his Catholic secondary school, Fr Ez. Fr Ez had taught his pupils a lot about other religions as well as Catholicism and one of the more exotic ones Kelly remembered was voodoo and how bizarrely in Cuba that many voodoo gods had been paired with Catholic saints so that Cubans could carry out their voodoo rituals behind the cloak of also being Catholics at the same time. He also had a brief recollection of a scandal caused by Pope John Paul II who had visited a voodoo snake house when he had visited the African country of Benin. Cuba was still as much a voodoo country as a Catholic one. Kelly had that unerring feeling that there might be lots of forces to contend with in the days to come and some of which he may not have ever encountered before.

As Kelly started off again towards the exit he glanced to the side and saw a woman cleaner with a mop. Her movements were very slow but methodic. Her face was pale and her eyes looked lifeless. For a split second Kelly felt as though the woman was watching him but with a firm shrug of his shoulders he strode confidently to the exit.

Eleven

FLOXLY was in the office of the Foreign Secretary Douglas Cummings. Floxly and Cummings worked well together and they had shared several security-related close shaves in the time since Floxly had become Prime Minister. After several reports on Jack Kelly turned out to have been misleading they had commissioned a 'Positive Vetting' report on Kelly by one of the most experienced civil servants in Whitehall. The report had been put to one side during the recent comings and goings in Uzbekistan since Floxly had watched Kelly closely as he had brokered a major deal between the British and the Russians leading him for once not to question Kelly's allegiance.

Kelly's past especially his time in Moscow in the 1990's was very colourful and the only true fact that everyone agreed on was that he had turned down MI6's attempts to recruit him more than once. He and his wife had lived in a rented dacha in a village outside Moscow called Barvihka during their time in Moscow. Barvihka was the former KGB area which had been transformed into the Russian Beverley Hills by rich oligarchs. Kelly had worked initially against and then increasingly on behalf of many Russians who had gone onto become very powerful and Kelly's allegiance had become very much a topic of debate or on several occasions, a real source of concern. No one yet had tied down the full facts about Kelly let alone how he thought and who he might or might not be working for.

The civil servant had, however, brought the final draft of his report in order to tidy up the loose ends of his assignment and Floxly and Cummings both confirmed that they had read it carefully. The civil servant was hoping to put the report to bed and move on to more interesting work.

"There is only one minor point still as far as I am concerned," said Floxly. "Do we know why he chose to study Russian at university?"

The civil servant raised his eyebrows and then looked at his notes which were much thicker than the report he had given Floxly and Cummings. "I am not sure," he said, "other than a comment he gave to his professor at university, that 'his grandfather had wished he could speak Russian so that he could understand what the communist infiltrators in the unions at the docks in Liverpool in the 1950's and 1960's were saying'."

"What do you think that means?"

"No idea, frankly," replied the civil servant.

"Well, perhaps you should add that question to your list of final loose ends," said Floxly with a smile.

"Of course," replied the civil servant, "and there is perhaps one more point," he said again looking at his notes, "which may follow on from this."

"Go on," said Floxly raising an eyebrow.

"Well, this is the grandfather on his mother's side who also had a son."

"An uncle then to Kelly," said Cummings who had remained quiet so far.

"Yes. He was ten years older than Kelly's mother. He had a short career in the Army with active service in North Africa before he emigrated in the early 1960's."

Floxly and Cummings looked at each other.

"Where to?" asked Cummings.

"To the US," replied the civil servant.

There was a short silence. Positive Vetting reports rarely throw up anything interesting or noteworthy about a subject's parents or siblings. It was often the wider family members or friends who can have a great influence over a subject without anyone noticing and worryingly such people are often able to stay under the radar.

"And what more do we know about this uncle and any contact with Kelly?" asked Floxly slowly.

"He worked in Detroit and I can enquire further with the US agencies, if you wish," replied the civil servant. "We believe that he was involved with the Amercian Armed Forces since a reference was requested from the UK regiment he served in."

"Why don't we do that," said Floxly with a forced smile. Such enquiries ought to have been done as soon as such a potentially pivotal figure in Kelly's life was identified especially one who it seemed had a link to the US military.

The civil servant nodded and managed to stifle a sigh. The work on the report had been painstaking and exhaustive. He had hoped that it would now have been completed but it was now clear to him that in the eyes of both Cummings and Floxly his 'vetting' report was positively not finished.

Twelve

KELLY relaxed slighlty in the short taxi ride from the airport to the Hotel Park View in La Habana Vieja, the old town area of Havana. His mind flicked back briefly to the Spanish people he had met in Moscow. In declining to take them on as a client in favour of the large US agricultural company, Millingtons, when it became known that both companies were interested in acquiring a stake in the same Russian sugar beet collective farm, his firm had made an astute choice. The Spanish, it had emerged later, had got themselves into a bit of bother over the exhibition of maps and coins and Kelly had never found out the real reasons why. Such incidents were common place in those days in Moscow. Potential investors in Russia at the time ranged from royalty and super wealthy families to criminals from all over the place. Deciding who to work for was as crucial and deciding which investment deals to try to put together.

Kelly had chatted in decent Spanish to the taxi driver on the journey. Although speaking in Spanish, the Cuban driver sounded very different from the Spanish people Kelly had known. There were more differences than just the accent but Kelly could not quite work them out. As the taxi pulled up outside the hotel, a seven-storey restored colonial building with distinctive green walls, the driver turned to Kelly, smiled and said:

"You will have a good time in our country, senor, if, as some people here say, Havana is not your last stop."

"It wont be," replied Kelly handing over the fare and a large tip. "Hopefully I'll be visiting other parts of the country."

After the long day Kelly had had he decided to have dinner in his hotel and soon after checking-in he went down to the hotel's restaurant. The restaurant was full but the manager said that he could fit Kelly in around 9pm. Kelly has just over an hour to wait and so he decided to take a stroll. The hotel concierge explained that there were plenty of bars in the old town and that his best option was to look into several to find the one he liked the look of the best. Kelly thanked the concierge and as he headed across the lobby to the glass doors of the entrance he heard a familiar sound. Low but methodical. A hotel cleaner was mopping the lobby floor. Her face was pale, her eyes a dull grey. Kelly shuddered momentarily. There seemed to be a striking resemblance to the cleaner at the airport but then Kelly smiled. Why should he be surprised? The abiding characteristic of workers under communist rule of whatever form was the uniformity of dress and look. Clearly Cuban cleaners would look like this one wherever they worked.

Kelly headed through the narrow streets of the old town and soon found himself in one of the main bar areas. Kelly always tried to avoid the tourist traps and quickly discounted a string of bars with signs in English promising the true Havana experience which seemed to boil down to cheap rum punches and disco-sounding salsa dancing. As he walked a little further he caught sight of two old men playing dominoes outisde of a bar in a small side street and as dominoes is one of the main pastimes of genuine Cubans he decided he would try this particular bar. And also when in Havana he smiled to himself he would have to have some rum, some Havana Club, Cuba's most famous brand.

He stepped ito the bar and was immediately disappointed. Except for another two old men at a table in the corner the bar was empty. Its décor was authentic enough with dark wood panels, old framed photographs and sawdust on the floor. Behind the bar were an assortment of bottles of local rums and on the bar was a pump of local beer. There was no music which again was a disappointment but there was a low hum of someone singing probably in a neighbouring bar or building. The bartender nodded to him and he ordered a Havana Club. A large measure was poured in a tumbler for him in silence.

Kelly stood at the bar and took a taste. It was earthy with a hint of sugar and strong. He breathed in deeply and then caught the aroma of a burning flower as well as the rum. He turned to look at the two old men and lifted his glass in a mini toasting gesture. They did not smile at him and Kelly detected a challengng look in the eyes of one of the men who then made the slightest nod of his head and then flicked his eyes to the bartender and then to the doorway behind Kelly to the right of the bar. It was the quickest of movements and had Kelly not been highly trained in human observation techniques he would have missed it. Kelly could not tell whether it was meant as an invitation or as a warning but he turned around back to the bar, downed the rest of his rum and walked to the doorway.

Kelly walked through the doorway and saw two doors and a flight of steps. The singing he had heard was now getting louder and drumbeats had started, one low and slow and one higher and faster. He went down the steps. His brain had gone into overdrive as he tried to understand the singing and also to work out the aroma which was becoming pungent and increasingly like an incense. A door at the bottom of the steps was slightly ajar and a dim light was seeping out. He wished he had had a few more rums but thinking back to Fr Ez and his lessons on exotic religious practices he pushed the door and stepped in.

This time he was not disappointed. He was shocked. Both his hands were quickly taken hold of by very soft hands and he was guided in, the door closing shut behind him. He was handed a dark glass and he drank its contents in one large swig. He was given a chair and he sat down, his body numbing but his brain buzzing.

In the centre of the room was a wide wooden throne covered in a bright red cloth. A man and woman were seated on the throne. They were dressed in multicoloured robes and covered in several long necklaces of beads. They had elaborate headdresses on their heads. They were made of animal skulls and horns and were decorated in red ribbons of silk. The man held a long sword, the woman a short rod with feathers on the end. There was a wooden box on the floor in front of them. In a corner of the room there was a small area coordoned off by a screen made of the same bright red cloth as on the throne.

The singing he had heard had now changed into a low and monotonous chant made by the twenty or so other people in the room. They were a mix of men and women and largely very dark-skinned. Kelly listened to the chant to see if he could make out any of the words but as he did an eeire silence descended as the man in the robe stood up. He circled the wooden box and then started to shout at the people in the room. There was venom and bile in his voice as he pointed at various individuals and after each harangue he would point to the wooden box. After five minutes or so he stopped shouting and the chant began again. Bottles with a dark liquid inside were passed from hand to hand and swigged with gusto.

Then the drums started again and one by one the people began to dance. The dance was manic and within minutes bodies were drenched in sweat and the dance movements shifted from manic to delerious and further to losses of control over legs and arms. Bodies then writhed and crawled across the floor moving over each other. Eyes sparked with a deep black intensity and tongues hissed. When it seemed as though everyone would pass out the man banged the handle of his sword on the floor and everywhere went silent. The woman stood up and walked over and into the coordoned-off area.

A minute later she emerged. She led a white goat with red ribbons tied around its ears on a rope and was followed by a girl in a pristine white robe and with the same red ribbons in her hair. The woman led them to the wooden box and then began a bizarre dance of her own. She moved around in a circle on one leg and sang to the box as if it were a new born baby. Kelly could hear her voice but could not work out any of the words. After a couple of minutes she stopped and prostrated herself in front of the box. The man then stood up, screamed a blood-curdling scream as if to the heavens and then he opened the box. With an audible slither and rasping hiss a four-foot long green snake slid out of the box. As if all poleaxed at once the other people fell to the floor and prostrated themselves as the woman had done. Kelly felt his body jump as if to lay down on the floor with everyone else but his legs and feet would not move. The snake moved quickly and went around the goat and the girl in a tight circle.

At that point the man screamed again. His tone this time of unbridled joy and triumph. People jumped up, the drums beat and the dancing began again. This time men and women were writhing together, bodies entwining, moans pulsing and all the time the green snake circled the goat and girl. Kelly closed his eyes but no matter how hard he tried to keep them shut he was watching more and more vivid and debauched scenes from the underworld unravel before him. His fascination overtook his normal revulsion at such wanton degeneration in human behaviour.

After what seemed an eternity Kelly felt himself being lifted up and then he was outside the bar. The air was cool. There was a taxi waiting and he got in. Kelly would never be sure if the next thirty minutes happened or were in his mind. The driver turned and smiled at him. He had a wild smile on his face and he literally began to drive like a man possessed.

The taxi's tyres screeched violently as the driver set off. He raced down Calle Habana, turned left and then right and then stopped at a traffic light. Kelly could see the grand building of the Museo de la Revolucion at the next corner. The taxi was headed for the Malecon, the wide avenue along the coast but just as the driver banged his foot on the accelerator a baseball bat shattered the windscreen and gunshots filled the air. A cold sweat poured down Kelly's back as his door was pulled open and a scantily-dressed young woman in clear distress jumped in.

"Drive!" she screamed to the driver who was brushing shards of glass off himself. He banged his foot on the accelerator again and the taxi flew off. Bullets then raked the back of the taxi. Kelly managed to dive down in his seat grabbing the young woman only to find that he was holding a lifeless body and that his hands were covered in sticky blood. A large truck loomed ahead of the taxi and then slammed into the front of the taxi. The other passenger side door was flung open and the body of the young woman was dragged out by two men. Their faces were contorted with anger and as Kelly tried to make himself as small as possible one of the men lifted a revolver and fired three shots into the back of the taxi driver. The driver slumped forward but then the taxi was thrust into reverse. The taxi driver turned round and smiled wickedly at Kelly. The three bullets had gone straight through him and had punctuated his shoulders and back like bullets going through a target at a shooting range.

Before the next corner the taxi took a sharp turn down what seemed to be a blind alley but the driver continued down it and then drove through a wooden gate which opened for them just as they arrived. The taxi stopped in a large courtyard. There were only a few lights on. Kelly surveyed the courtyard and as he peered more and more deeply into the dim light bodies appeared all around sitting or laying on the ground. Needles were everywhere, a thick smoke was rising and gradually the bodies started to moan as much as in pain as in pleasure.

And then a crack of a whip and into the courtyard ran a man frantically looking for somewhere to run. His eyes locked onto Kelly's and Kelly had to shut his eyes tight to avoid the man's look of absolute fear burning straight through his eyes into his brain. The man yelped pitifully as the whip cracked again and then a swarm of armed men surrounded the man. In an almost theatrical perfomance, ballet-like even, the whip was flicked around the man's neck and with a supernatural strength the holder of the whip pulled the man forwards, threw the whip over an overhanging branch of a tree and the man was hanged in a second. As the man's legs twitched in the air the taxi reversed again. Kelly felt his stomach rise sharply, saliva flood his mouth and then a huge explosion and darkness.

The sound of waves crashing onto the shore became louder and louder and Kelly opened his eyes. His brain was flooded with frozen images from the dancing and of the taxi ride. Then the sound of a gun going off and he shot up to find himself sitting on an outcrop of rocks below a concrete wall. He shook his head and then closed his eyes slowly. The image in his mind made him jump to his feet, climb over the wall onto an embankement and then to try and run, to run away from himself. It was the image of a huge green snake with smiling eyes and its forked tongue hissing which in a flash mutated into the olive-skinned face of a dark-haired and sultry woman with sparkling eyes and immensely sensual lips and then in another flash into the stern beauty of a blond-haired woman he instantly recognised as Anna, the FSB agent. Then in the next flash the image exploded into thousands of tiny pieces. Hallucinations like this were never in the plan, he had to get control of himself. He started to run and run.

Thirteen

IT was that time of the evening when the bars in the old town were filling up with people, smoke and noise. It was a coolish evening but Gifford, although only wearing a shirt and jeans, was sweating profusely. As he entered El Bar del Diablo he realised why he had made such a conscious decision to change his normal dress. Behind the bar he recognised the gruesome doll with a beard and green cardigan. It was hanging from the rope. Gifford instintively put his hand to his neck at which point the bartender signalled to him to go through the bar and out of the back door and into the dark alley. The two men who had threatened Gifford in Miami stepped out of the shadows and into the pale beam of light which came from a dim lamppost in the alley. The first man smiled and his mouth seemed to sparkle.

"So, just can't stop gambling?" he said with a wheeze which accentuated the rasp in his voice. "Have you got the money?"

Gifford took a step forward and moved his right arm from behind his back. In a flash the second man jumped over and thrust a knife towards Gifford's chest. Seeing a small wooden box in Gifford's hand he stopped as the tip of his knife touched Gifford's throat and he pulled back the knife slightly.

"These are some of my wife's jewellery and they are worth a lot more than what I owe," said Gifford with a composure that surprised even him. The beads of sweat on his forehead had increased into what looked like tears streaming down his cheeks.

"Let me see," said the first man tearing the box from Gifford's hand and signalling to the second man to put his knife back up to Gifford's throat.

The man looked at the box. It had the outline of an old map of part of an island and in the corner was a family crest. The crest showed a pile of gold coins with a snake wrapped around them.

"This is not the one we were told about," said the man looking at Gifford with a frown. "This is much smaller."

"A woman of her wealth has several jewellery boxes," replied Gifford. This was true and Gifford was hoping that his wife would not miss this one straight away. She kept it in a drawer and had not worn its content for several months. "Let me open it," continued Gifford.

The first man reluctantly handed it back and Gifford looked intently at the lock on the front of the box. There was a small keyhole and Gifford had forgotten to find and to bring the key. He fumbled with the lock.

"What are you doing?" said the man. A sense of panic left Gifford and seemed to flow into the two other men. Without warning the second man grabbed the box and knocked Gifford to the ground.

"He is playing with us," said the second man his body shaking. He knelt down and banged the box on the floor. There was a dull crack and then with his knife the second man split the box open. He pulled out a long pearl necklace and held it up to the dim light.

The first man studied the necklace and let out a small whistle under his breath. "If these are real, then your debts are settled for now," he said with a rasp.

Gifford was shaking on the floor. He was literally gambling that they would let him live so that he could continue betting. The second man threw the box into the alley. He seemed to be aiming for a specific spot where it was much darker. Without another look at Gifford the two men went back into the bar.

A few moments later Gifford stood up and breathing deeply made his way in the direction of where the box had been thrown. As he stepped into the darknesss a heavy punch to his stomach sent him reeling back towards the bar. He stumbled towards the back door to the bar and then threw himself down his back to the wall at the side of the door. His neck throbbed and as he grabbed his neck he felt a jabbing pain all around his throat. His assailant had not followed him but strode off deeper into the darkness.

A couple of streets away the assailant stopped alongside a car, opened the back passenger door and got in. Another man was seated in the other back seat of the car.

"Let me see the box, Pavel," said the man taking the box. He looked at it carefully and smiled. "A crude copy but the gold coins and the snake are the same." He then took out a mobile phone and dialled. It was answered on the second ring. "Hello, boss," said the man, "I am returning your call."

"Very good, Vadim," replied Zelinsky who was in his office in the Lubyanka, the Headquarters of the FSB in Moscow. He stood up and walked to the door to his office which he closed. "What news?" asked Zelinsky.

"We have matched the signs and can confirm that the item acquired in Moscow is genuine," came back the reply.

"Very good," replied Zelinsky, "but please remember all of the objectives of your mission."

"Of course, and I will call again soon." With that Vadim Nazarov ended the call and looked again at the box. The snake was so distinct and was indeed almost a perfect copy of the emblem on the map.

Fourteen

KELLY finally stopped running. As the initial fright at the vision had subsided he had slowed and begun to look around himself. He was well practised in orienteering and he had taken part in a number of advanced exercises to find a way out of a hostile environment. He had paced his run and steadied his breathing and heart rate. He had had no way of calculating how far he was from his hotel. The bar had not been far but then he really did not know what had actually happened since. He had looked for some of the buildings he had set as points of references on his way to the hotel when he had arrived and when he had set out on his stroll. He spied a distinctive tower on a building and came to a halt.

The clock was showing that it was just after eight o'clock. Kelly looked around himself to confirm. By the sunlight and early morning heat he knew it was eight o'clock in the morning. He had lost the best part of twelve hours! This was so reminiscent of his time in Moscow. Business trips to Russian factories were more often than not based around the obligatory vodka-drinking sessions which could sometimes last for a couple of days before the Russians would engage in any serious discussions. Once in Perm Kelly had had to drink at lunchtime and at dinnertime for four days before the factory managers would even allow him to see past the factory's canteen let alone discuss potential investment in the factory.

Rather than now rely on his very hazy memory he decided to take the easy option. He checked that he still had his wallet which he did and he flagged down a taxi. The taxi was a stretched Lada model, a car made in Russia. Even though it was old and battered it would not have looked out of place in Moscow in the 1990's, Kelly thought to himself. For a split second as the taxi driver turned around in the cab Kelly had a vision of the manic taxi driver from the night before whom Kelly now remembered having an almost zombie-like face but this driver was much younger and had a pleasant smile.

Five minutes later Kelly was back in his hotel room. A message had been pushed under his door. Kelly picked it up and opened it. It was an address which had been sent to the hotel for his attention by fax and Kelly recalled what he had been told when he had been in transit in Grand Cayman. He had had a call from Floxly's PA to warn him about using phones in Cuba. When Cuba's telecoms company, Empresa de Telecomunicaciones de Cuba S.A., had been partially privatised much mirth had been caused by the huge number of people on the company's payroll and the minister's answer to the question as to why so many - 'Because of all the calls we have to monitor and listen in on,' had replied the minister in all honesty. Floxly's PA had suggested that Kelly seek out the British Consul at his apartment and to avoid the British Embassy if possible. She would get the address to him once she had alerted the Consul.

Kelly showered and then had a quick coffee in the hotel bar. He studied a map and soon located the address. The apartment was on Calle 26 in the Miramar district, the fashionable residential area on the west side of Havana. The area contained many stately mansions several of which had been converted to embassies. Kelly made a mental note of the locations of the British and Russian embassies. Kelly took another taxi and as it stopped at a set of traffic lights Kelly studied a row of shops. He was struck by the lack of colour in the displays and then again by the pale face of a female shopkeeper. The eyes though lifeless seemed to be watching him.

When he arrived at the apartment Kelly rang the doorbell twice. The rings echoed loudly in the corridor and at the same time Kelly heard footsteps coming to the door. They were light but precise. The door opened and Kelly's eyebrows were immediately raised but fortunately he was able to quickly suppress the look on his face.

"Si?" said the woman who had opened the door. She was in a short cream dress and matching slippers. She had thick dark hair tied up under a clip and a silver necklace and pendant around her neck. The dress, slippers, hair and pearls all did only one thing - they accentuated the woman's natural beauty with just a hint of sophistication. Her face was a perfect oval, her skin a light shiny brown, her nose softly pointed, her eyes deep and brown and then her lips. Her lips drew all eyes to them – deeply red and mesmerising. She made everyone smile when they first set eyes upon her.

"Senora Thellwall-Jones?" asked Kelly who could not help himself from smiling.

"And might I ask who is asking," replied the woman speaking English with a husky Spanish lilt.

"My name is Jack. Jack Kelly," replied Kelly. "I believe this is Gifford Thellwall-Jones' apartment."

"It is," replied the woman opening the door further, "and I am his wife, Maria. Pleased to meet you, Jack Kelly," she continued offering Kelly her hand.

Kelly almost went to kiss her hand but stopped himself and shook her hand. Her hand was soft and warm.

"Pleased to meet you, too, Maria," continued Jack. "I hope your husband was told of my coming?"

"He is in a business meeting," continued Maria, "but please come in. We shall have some tea or coffee if you prefer?"

Kelly said he would be very grateful for some tea and followed Maria into the apartment. The apartment was classically furnished. He went into the sitting room and Maria said she would see to some tea and left the sitting room. As Kelly watched her leave he shook his head. Her face had been so attractive and dazzling that he had missed the obvious. She looked very much like the Spanish woman who had almost become the client of his firm in Moscow. A woman who had accompanied her father whose family owned one of the largest sugar refineries in Spain and who had gotten into trouble with the exhibition of maps and coins. Was this déjà vu?

Before he could think any further Maria came back into the sitting room.

"Are you here on Embassy business?" asked Maria who motioned for Kelly to take a seat on a leather sofa. She put the tray on a table in front of the sofa and poured two cups of tea. Kelly had to admit to himself that Maria's movements and general poise were something to behold. He had never seen tea poured in such a sensual way before.

"Unofficially," replied Kelly, "I have been asked to liaise with Gifford on a particular matter."

"I understand," said Maria fixing Kelly with a gentle smile as she handed him a cup. "I suggest that you go to the offices of Newgold this afternoon. I will give you the address. Gifford is going there after lunch and he will be there for the rest of the day."

"Thank you," replied Kelly enjoying his cup of tea. "Am I correct in thinking that you are perhaps Spanish?" Kelly was a linguist and a trained one at that. Post his studies he had undergone some intensive and specialist training on accents to develop his listening and aural recognition skills. Underneath the language blanket of any key language such as English, Spanish and Russian lie a myriad of regional variances and identifying the precise initial location of a person's speech was a major advantage in working out where a person came from and potentially from that what he or she might be doing in a particular situation.

Maria looked at Kelly with another gentle smile. "You are," she replied and turned her head slightly to look at a painting which hung in pride of place over the sitting room mantelpiece. Kelly's eyes followed hers.

"May I?" asked Kelly starting to stand up.

"Be my guest," replied Maria.

Kelly approached the painting. It was of a middle-aged man dressed in seventeenth-century Spanish finery. He was standing on the edge of a dock with tall ships in the background. There was a barrel containing bright gold coins next to him. Kelly read the name attached on a small wooden plaque at the bottom of the frame of the painting.

"Xavier Fernandez de la Pena," said Kelly. "The de la Pena's who mined so much gold in South America in the seventeenth and eighteenth centuries?" Kelly now definitely had that unsettling feeling that there was a link between Maria and his time in Moscow.

"You know the history well, Mr Kelly," replied Maria her voice rising ever so slightly, as if a touch nervous.

Kelly decided to stick to what he knew about the family's history and to avoid mentioning Moscow.

"A little," replied Kelly looking again at the painting and then at a family crest in the top corner. It had a pile of gold coins guarded by a dragon which on closer inspection would turn out to be a large green snake. "Did the family not lose several ships of gold in the late 1600's when they were on the way to Spain?"

"Our family did," replied Maria opening a small wooden box on the table and taking out a cigarette which she lit. She pointed to the box but Kelly shook his head. "We lost more than most."

"But the family still prospered?" said Kelly.

"Yes, we diversified over decades and became heavily involved in sugar cane," replied Maria who seemed to have recovered her composure. "But all that was a very, very long time ago. My family has lived off its property investments for many years now and I prefer a much more relaxed and sociable lifestyle."

Kelly had lots of questions bubbling in his brain but he had a job to do first. He would meet Gifford, find out what he could about the death of the geologist and then hope he would meet Maria again to perhaps revisit the topic. There was one question, though, that he thought would not do any harm.

"Was there not one famous galleon, the Santa Monica, carrying gold doubloons from Peru on its way to Spain which took shelter in Cuba before sadly running aground?" asked Kelly with a smile. "I think the story went by the name of 'Last Stop Havana' because Havana sadly became its last stop because it ran aground further along the coast, although there were rumours that some of its cargo may have been saved. Cadiz in Spain was meant to be its last stop."

"Such rumours," replied Maria taking another cigarette from the box on the table and lighting it. "Such rumours come and go from time to time but, believe me, my family's ancestors searched and searched for years. The searches especially off the west coast killed several senior members of my family. We had to accept that the gold was lost for good."

Maria exhaled and smiled at Kelly with a brief intensity which hit Kelly like a flash of lightning. He coughed and smiled back. For some reason he was not convinced that Maria, who he could feel had the charm to wrap any man around her little finger, believed herself what she had just said. He smiled again and then dropped his eyes ever so slighlty to avert the gaze which she had fixed upon him through the small rings of smoke she had made as she had exhaled.

Kelly felt a wisp of smoke across his face and as his eyes stang ever so slightly he could see the exhibition in the Kempinksi Hotel in Moscow and the real piles of ancient gold ingots and doubloons that had been put on display to such dramatic effect underneath the centrepiece of the exhibition - the secretly-copied map, 'La Carta del Oro Oculto', as Kelly's memory focused on the map and he finally remembered its title – the 'Map of Hidden Gold' as it was translated on the display sign. Kelly could still feel the effect of the display – the brightest and warmth of the gold lit up and seemed to heat the room whilst outside it was dark and freezing in a very, very cold January in Moscow.

Back in his hotel with several hours to wait before making his way to the Newgold office Kelly decided it was time to get back on task. The visit with Maria had flooded his brain with numerous thoughts of a positive nature which thankfully had displaced the jagged and bewildering visions from the previous evening. He thought of a possible way to get back on track – a method he used so often in the past. Local newspapers. Local newspapers especially in cities where life was changing so fast were a wealth of information. In Russia in the mid 1990's when the press became very free as censorship was dismantled for several years almost anything was published from genuine news stories to downright lies. Now as Cuba evolved and despite the growing popularity and freeing up of the Internet, newspapers still had a role to play as a source of information.

He picked up a bunch of newspapers from the concierge's desk and set to scanning any article which looked interesting. He had learned to speed-read very fast and was proficient in several languages including Spanish. Having discarded the English language paper, The Havana Times, he concentrated on two newspapers in Spanish.

After several minutes he took stock on what he had discovered. There were two contrasting events of political importance and then exactly what he had been looking for. The events were diametrically opposed. On one hand the Russians had launched a military cooperation exercise with the Cuban Armed Forces. The precise details were unclear but the objective was stated as the detection and capturing of international smugglers on land, sea and air. To Kelly this looked like a not very subtle cover story. Opposing this was the rise in pro-US movements. Groups both in Cuba and Florida were rumoured to preparing to hold public meetings and rallies to show support for the Cuban Exiles and their long-cherished aim of returning Cuba to the American sphere of influence. Again hardly a convincing cover story, thought Kelly. Floxly's words about possible Russian and American activities in Cuba came straight back to Kelly.

But back to task. On an inside page of the Tribuna de La Havana newspaper he found a short article on the UK geologist, Darren Smith, who worked for Newgold. The Havana Chief of Police was believed to be on the point of launching a formal murder investigation. 'So,' thought Kelly, 'the death is very suspicious after all.' The final line of the article as to the reason why was the information Kelly had been hoping for. The reason for investigating the death was the suspicion that the geologist's latest work and map data was missing. Kelly folded up the newspaper. Next stop Newgold.

As he passed the concierge's desk on his way to the lifts a brightly-coloured leaflet took his eye. It was an invitation to a hotel tour on Friday evening to the Plaza Vieja. Payment would be taken on the evening. Kelly took one leaflet and then another. He was not sure why. As he walked away from the desk the hotel cleaner he had seen previously stepped in front of him and nodded slightly to him. Kelly shuddered at the sadness in her eyes.

Fifteen

THE Canadians had a rented office in the Vedado district of Havana near the Plaza de la Revolucion. In addition to two Directors, Bill Trump, the C.E.O., and John Dow, the Director of Strategy, they had an experienced geologist and a support team of three Canadian staff. Partly due to costs and partly due to their desire to build goodwill in Havana they employed some thirty locals, a dozen or so in their office and the rest as field teams to take the ex-pat staff around Havana and more importantly around the island as the geologist and his team made some studies in the locations which CCMC had identified as the ones they were interested in. The company was building a good reputation.

Dow had asked to have a private meeting with Trump and they were in the small office which Trump used and had his name and title as C.E.O. written on an A4-sized piece of paper and attached to the door with bluetack.

"What is your general feeling for the shortlist?" asked Dow, his American accent becoming stronger as he was speaking in private.

"I am sure we will be on the list," replied Trump, "and we are concentrating on the deposits in the west. Our team is convinced that these are the two best concessions."

"And the other bidders?" asked Dow.

"Hard to say. There seems to be interest in all six concessions but people are being very cagey in public, as you would expect. We are though meeting the Brits for dinner as soon as the shortlist is announced to share some information with them. The only major company which we don't recognise or work with is Cyprus Gold and we have no idea what they are are up to. Look a dodgy bunch."

"Well, if we can square something with the Brits, then I would be very hopeful," replied Dow. He knew full well that the Russians were behind Cyprus Gold but preferred to leave the mining executive in the dark. He was after all on the Board of Directors of CCMC as their political fixer as well as directing strategy. There was one issue though which he needed to involve Trump in and it was time to start.

"I have some information," continued Dow, "which is a little left-field but might be worth adding to what we already know."

"Really?" replied Trump. He had been briefed by the major shareholder in CCMC that Dow's roles were not traditional but that they could well contribute to the success of CCMC which was all Trump cared about especially as his remuneration depended on CCMC being as successful as possible. Canadians did well in Cuba and CCMC had given the appearance of being Canadian in public very well.

"Yes, it is old information but it may have some insights which geological and geographic studies do not provide." As he said this Dow took out a large piece of paper from a tube and unfolded it and placed it on the desk between them. It was an A3-sized photocopy of an old map. It was of a part of an island and had an elaborate compass in a corner.

"It is a photocopy of a map from the seventeenth century which we acquired from a source in Miami but which originated here on the island and then was hidden in Europe literally for hundreds of years. It is one of several hand-made copies of an original," said Dow.

"How does this help us?" asked Trump studying the map intently.

"I am assured that it will but I am not entirely sure yet how," said Dow. He knew pretty well what the map could tell them but he had to take it one step at a time. "I was told that it reveals the sites of old gold mines from the sixteenth and seventeen centuries which fell into dissue many, many years ago. Many of their locations have also been obscured by mine tunnels collapsing and by earthquakes. Cuba has had its share of large earthquakes over the last four hundered years, as you know. They have reached over 7 on the Richter scale and large parts of Santiago have been damaged several times. The way to find out if there are any such hidden mines is to compare this ancient map with more modern maps. An old mine may still have gold deposits which nowadays might well be economically or technologically viable to exploit."

Trump looked puzzled. As an experienced mining executive this map did not look convincing. It was something you would expect to see at Disney World on the Pirates of the Caribbean attraction, he thought to himself.

"Can I suggest," continued Dow his tone acquiring a certain hardness, "that you ask our geologist perhaps with the help of a cartographer to study it, compare it to our maps and see if anything pops up?"

Trump did not reply for a moment and then replied. "I do not see why not. It is intriguing, if nothing else. Historical information can often be valuable."

Dow nodded and left.

Dow's call to Langley shortly after was brief and in code and simply stated that the game was on.

Sixteen

IN stark contrast to CCMC Cyprus Gold had not hired any local staff and their office was little more than a letter box on the wall of an old colonial building in a street in the centre of Havana. In addition though they did have a basement room in the same building. A flight of steps led down to an unmarked door to the basement. Anna had made the mistake of following Vadim Nazarov and Pavel Varonsky, the two Directors of Cyprus Gold, after they had had a briefing meeting at the Lincoln Hotel where Anna was staying. In the meeting Anna had been told the company only had the letter box as it needed an address on the island and that she should use the facilities of the hotel's business centre to do her job as press officer.

Nazarov and Varonsky had not thought for a moment that Anna would find their basement room. When she had tried the door handle the pair in a flash had unceremoniously yanked the door open, grabbed Anna and hurled her across the floor. As Anna looked up and moved her long blond hair out of her face she was staring down the barrels of two pistols which she instantly recognised as a Glock and a Makarov.

"Well, well," said Nazarov with a grin, "look who has found our room, Pavel."

There was a tense silence. Anna's handbag was out of reach but thankfully it was still zipped up and her handgun concealed inside.

"We told you to work in the hotel," said Varonsky gruffly. Nazarov was obviously in charge and Varonsky sounded to Anna to be no more than a brutish enforcer which again was just what he looked like. Narazov on the other hand looked more like a highly polished diplomat. When she had been presented to the pair, she had had a letter of support from the Russian Ministry for Economic Development and she was pretty sure that the pair had bought the cover story but the next few seconds would be very critical.

She thought back to her advanced combat training and how to use the art of surprise even with guns pointed at her. She made her decision. She ignored all her training and burst into tears. Both men laughed and watched as Anna started to scramble to her feet.

Nazarov nodded to Varonsky who with a grunt went to grab hold of Anna's right hand. Anna let him and levered herself upright as Varonsky's eye lingered on Anna's dishevelled skirt and long legs. That gave Anna the split second she needed and with a shocked glance at Nazarov she slapped Varonsky across his face. She did not slap hard but Varonsky yelped in surprise and Nazarov laughed loudly.

"Don't you ever try to touch me," shouted Anna crying again. She looked like a pathetic young woman defending herself against a potential attack.

"Stop, Pavel," said Nazarov. Varonsky's face had reddened deeply and not from the force of the slap which had almost been like an acting slap. He was staring at Anna with an obvious intention in mind. "She is a feisty one and a well brought-up woman from Moscow. You can keep to the local women for your fun."

"Thank you," said Anna quickly and picking up her bag and taking out a tissue. She now had very easy access to her handgun and felt in control. "I should not have come here and I will forget I was ever here."

"No, need," replied Nazarov who seemed to be trying to impress Anna. "You need to know a few things."

Anna looked at Nazarov with the most innocent and bimbo-ish look she could manufacture. "Really?" she replied.

"As long, of course, as you keep quiet."

"Of course," replied Anna looking around the room. There was a table with more weapons on it and what looked like plastic bags with US dollars inside, several chairs and crates. In a corner there was a sink and a cupboard with several bottles of vodka and some basic food on it.

"Take a seat," said Nazarov. "And Pavel, why don't you fetch some food from one of the bars on the street." It was a clear order and Varonsky nodded and left but not without a scowl at Anna.

"You must continue talking to everyone here, especially the Cubans and the press, making the case for us as the real friends of Cuba ready to invest big time on the island, " said Nazarov who had also sat down. To Anna what he was saying was easy to recognise as an FSB-style briefing so she interrupted him several times with inane and silly questions to appear to be as dumb as possible. The line Nazarov gave her was very subtle. They were ex-KGB agents who were working again for the KGB-turned-FSB on a confidential basis. Anna widened her eyes on the mention of KGB and looked quickly around the room as if expecting someone to be spying on them. She gave the look of being mightily impressed by Nazarov who soaked up the flattery. Their work for the FSB did involve trying to win the gold concessions and indeed they were going much futher and were aiming to cash in on some 'gold chips' of their own. At this point Anna feigned great confusion and Nazarov just laughed and then whispered quietly that 'Anna need not worry and just to think of it of a kind of treasure hunt.' Anna nodded back wide-eyed again as a whole new train of thoughts kicked off in her brain.

Nazarov finished with his 'coup de grace'. He and Varonsky who was much more able than he might look, even knew President Bunin and he reckoned that they were about the only two people who were involved with the FSB who did not fear Bunin.

"Bunin will never fight with us," said Nazarov reaching the climax of his pep talk, "we know things about him that no one else knows. He has even asked us to take care of some other projects while we are here."

"Wow," whispered Anna, her incredulity worthy of a Hollywood actress. "Other projects?"

"All I can say is other metals and some other deals so if you see us acting in different ways do not look surprised. You are the public face of Cyprus Gold and you will concentrate on the gold concessions. When it is all over, then if you have done your job," Nazarov paused and fixed Anna with a look intended to chill her to the core. She absorbed the threat immediately but looked back with startled eyes. "If you have done your job, then I will let you share some of our other benefits."

At that point the door to the basement opened and Varonsky came in carrying a tray with plates of what looked like fried eggs and potatoes.

"Will you join us for lunch, Anna?" asked Nazarov.

"I would like to go back to the hotel," replied Anna with a waver in her voice.

"Very good," said Nazarov with a smile. He felt very satisfied with himself and was sure that Anna would now do as he said and he had to admit to himself that he thought she would be very good at it.

Anna left without looking back and Varonsky closed the door loudly behind her. Anna walked twenty or so paces and then stopped. She straightened up and her whole demeanour changed back to normal. She now had Nazarov and Varonsky where she wanted them. The only thought that niggled her was Nazarov's boast about not being afraid of Bunin and knowing something about him. She would have to remain super wary of Nazarov. Her next task was to find the other team that Zelinsky had told her would soon be on the ground and be working on the Russians' wider plan. Zelinsky had not told her any details of the wider plan but said it would become clear. Her prime task for now was to be eyes and ears on the ground and she was pleased that the last thirty minutes had created the access she needed for that.

As she set off she looked in the window of a food shop and caught sight of a female face. The display in the window she had to admit reminded her of her childhood in St Petersburg before the fall of Communism – faded cardboard photographs and no real food. She looked again expecting to see the face which had struck her as very sad, but the face had gone.

Seventeen

KELLY was impressed with the Newgold office. It was on the fifth floor of the Santiago building in the Miramar Trade Centre. The offices were some of the most modern in Havana having been built in the early 2000's and they would not look out of place in any modern city. Situated on the inland side of the coast road they had good views of the sea and the Malecon from the higher floors. Kelly had put on a jacket and a tie. He was met by a receptionist, a smartly-dressed young Cuban woman, whom he asked if he could see Gifford Thellwall-Jones. He did not have a specific appointment with Gifford but he had been assured by his office in London that Gifford had been contacted a few days before. The receptionist said she would go and find Mr Thellwall-Jones.

A few minutes later she was back and asked Kelly to follow her. She led him to a conference room which had glass walls and Kelly was able to spot three men in the room. As the receptionist opened the glass door a man came out closing the door behind him.

"You must be Jack Kelly. I am Gifford," said the man with a wince. He looked to be in a little pain and held his neck. "Bit of whiplash," he said rubbing his neck. "Must get it seen to shortly."

"Yes, I am Jack," said Kelly extending his hand. Gifford looked and sounded every bit a Foreign Office type to Kelly – relatively scruffily dressed though in expensive clothes and shoes, beard and the Queen's English for an accent. "I had the great pleasure of meeting your wife earlier," continued Kelly wondering how such a Spanish beauty could have fallen for a man like Gifford. Gifford must have had twenty years on Maria.

"Yes, she rang," replied Gifford.

"Did London contact you?" asked Kelly detecting a note of uncertainty in Gifford's voice.

"Yes," replied Gifford with an exaggerated nod of his head, "but I had better introduce you to the Newgold team now that you are here," he continued and opened the door to the conference room before Kelly could object. "Gentlemen," he said, "may I introduce Jack Kelly from London."

Kelly followed Gifford into the conference room and smiled at the two men who had stood up.

"Malcolm Raven," said the first man who was well dressed.

"Roger Swannel," said the second man who was more casually dressed.

"Pleased to meet you both," said Jack shaking hands with both warmly.

The next words to be spoken felt to Kelly as though a hand grenade had gone off next to him.

"What brings you to Cuba and more specifically to us?" asked Raven.

The question was as innocuous as any opening remark could have been but Kelly had not thought of this for a second. He had expected to meet Gifford and keep all his questions confidential. He could hardly tell a British company's two most senior executives that he been sent by the Prime Minister to make an off-the-record investigation into the now apparent murder of one of their key employees and to do it without involving the British Embassy. He had to think on his feet.

He had been taught well. They had called it 'functional improvisation' and he had to sound confident but only to a point. He could not overplay a story. He had to make his interlocutors part build the story themselves and above all he had to buy in their empathy.

"It is rather a delicate matter," he began lowering his voice ever so slightly. "Very delicate, I am afraid."

Raven and Swannel looked at each other. Swannel nodded slightly.

"Does it concern Smith?" asked Swannel.

Kelly nodded a couple of times quickly.

"How can we help?" asked Raven his tone already moving to an obliging, if overly polite, corporate-speak.

"I have been sent," replied Kelly with a grave look at Gifford, "on behalf of Smith's family. Or rather to be precise on behalf of the insurance company who underwrote his key man insurance policy."

"Of course, Roger," said Raven. "You normally deal with all those matters."

"That's great," continued Kelly. "Our firm wants to confirm some details as quickly as possible so that we can expedite the paperwork and authorise all claims under the policy and most importantly the life assurance payment to his family."

Kelly almost punched the air with his hand. His improvisation had been as clever as he could have hoped. He had them on side. He made a mental note to contact Floxly as soon as possible to have his story backed up. He decided to take it one step further.

"And I also have one request," said Kelly.

"Fire away," replied Raven.

"We prefer to work confidentially. Our firm knows Gifford and we were hoping that only he would know of our work here on the case," said Kelly quickly.

Raven frowned briefly. "That should not be a problem," he then said to Kelly's relief.

"Yes, I hate to say this but HMG's Foreign Office can often get in the way," continued Kelly, "if we have to go through official channels. If I can make a quick report and get it back to London, everything can work quickly indeed and that can only help Smith's family and hopefully the company."

"Agreed, Roger?" asked Raven.

Swannel nodded.

"Great," said Kelly. "Can you now give me some background on the company and then on what happened as you understand it?"

Raven gave a brief overview of Newgold. It had been established by some seasoned mining investors and raised a war chest of funds to invest in what Raven described as 'geologically challenging' deposits of scarce precious metals. They had identified a core list of potential deposits around the world and believed that their competitive edges were the expertise of their geologists, their experience in dealing with unruly governments and their ability to access new mining technology.

"But sadly, as you know," said Raven his tone turning grave, "we have just lost one of our top geologists."

"A replacement is on the way," added Swannel.

"And what do you know about any events leading up to this tragedy?" asked Kelly choosing his words carefully.

"Smith was a little highly-strung but brilliant at this work," replied Raven. "He had worked on a project in the Middle East for us before coming here. That project has to remain confidential as we are now in the final negotiating phase but his work in finding the best deposits there was first class."

"Was he a bit of a loner?" then asked Kelly probing the 'highly-strung' line.

"You could say that," replied Raven. "He worked best alone. Here he preferred the assistance of Gifford to get around the place and some of our locally-hired staff rather than the ex-pat team."

Kelly had almost forgotten about Gifford but he looked at him quizzically.

"He was a joy to assist," said Gifford with a slight cough and rubbing his neck.

Similar type, thought Kelly, both probably educated at Eton or another private school then Oxford or Cambridge.

"What was that taxi business all about, Gifford?" asked Swanell.

Kelly's ears pricked up. He had little information yet on the geologist's actual death other than a couple of lines in the local newspaper.

"A mix up. You know how disorganised this place can be," replied Gifford.

"The office ordered a taxi to pick Smith up but when it arrived he had already left and the taxi firm made quite a fuss about not getting the fare," interrupted Raven looking at Kelly with a heavy look.

"Do the police know?" asked Kelly.

"Yes," replied Raven, "and they said they would follow up if they thought it relevant."

To Kelly this was big news and he ran a multitide of scenarios through his mind. Was the geologist snatched? Was the taxi firm involved? Was someone inside Newgold involved? He would sit down later with a large blank piece of paper and start his own investigation. Gifford's throwaway comment also resonated in his brain. He turned to Gifford.

"How closely are you working with Newgold, Gifford?" he asked. Both Raven and Swannel looked at Kelly and for the first time there was a feeling of tension in the room.

"Our brief at the Foreign Office is to assist British companies as much as possible?" replied Gifford confidently.

"And on what basis?" pushed Kelly who had so much experience from Moscow of the Foreign Office doing precisely the opposite. In those days they never would never so much as even meet with a Britistsh company trying to do business in Russia. This had been is stark contrast to the US Embassy which went to great lengths to assist any US commercial venture in Russia.

"Some covering of expenses," replied Gifford now massaging his neck and avoiding glances.

Swannel looked at Raven with a very raised eyebrow.

"A consul's salary is way behind what one is paid in the private sector," continued Gifford in a tone almost more in protest than in explanation.

"And with such an expensive wife to support," said Raven with a warm smile. "I trust that we are covering your expenses sufficiently?"

Gifford nodded meekly. Kelly decided to let the point drop whilst mentally logging that Gifford was clearly as financially challenged as the company was geologically challenged. Kelly never believed in coincidences.

"And finally, if I may ask, what do you know about what actually happened to Smith?" asked Kelly.

Raven explained that all they knew was the finding of the body in the rocks off the Malecon. The initial theories of a mugging because of the disappearance of his briefcase had then turned into the bizarre claim of a ritual killing. A killing which had been further sensationalised into some form of voodoo ritual to appease an angry 'loa' as the locals called their voodoo gods.

"Was there anything important in his briefcase?" enquired Kelly remembering what he had read in the local newspaper.

"Not that we know of," replied Raven. "All his work is here in the office."

"Thank you," said Kelly surprised at the reply but making sure he did not let on that he potentially had information to the contrary and making a note to add Raven's assertion to his own investigation. "Well, there clearly is no doubt that this is a tragedy and there are no indications of suicide or other factors which could lead to the insurance payments being questioned."

"That's good to hear," said Raven. "Will you need to talk to anyone else?"

"I hope not. Our office in London has requested all the official files from the authorities here but I have enough from what you have kindly told me to expedite matters."

"Great," said Raven standing up and offering his hand. "And if you are still in town on in a couple of days' time why don't you join us for dinner? There will be a few other people from some of the other mining companies joining us and it may give you some more background. Time and place to be confirmed."

Kelly glanced at Gifford in an instant. Kelly saw that Gifford was about to object.

"Wonderful. I look forward to it." And with that he shook Raven's hand.

"And if you are interested the shortlist for the concessions will be announced at a press conference at the Ministry tomorrow."

"I'll try to make it," replied Kelly.

Back on the street Kelly walked briskly to the first café he could see and took a seat. He took out a sheath of A4 papers from his jacket pocket. It was a list of the delegates to the recent gold miming conference in Miami which he had 'acquired' from a table in the hotel at breakfast. He ran down the names of the delegates and companies. Several stood out through their names and nationalities but the one that Kelly focussed on the most was Newgold itself. His intuition would not let go. As he looked to the bar in the café for a waiter a pale-faced woman peered at him from behind the door into the café's kitchen. If Kelly had not become so used to pale faces of women everywhere he would have sworn that he was being watched.

Eighteen

THE second press conference at the Cuban Ministry for Energy and Mines was about to get underway. In contrast to the first press conference the audience this time was much larger and it was buzzing. Handshakes were vigorous as were nodded greetings. The atmosphere was friendly but tensions were rising. Over twenty mining companies were represented in the attendees but rumours were rife that the Cubans were taking the meaning of a shortlist literally. Lobbying had been intense over the last twenty-four hours with the Cuban Minister having been up all night in various restaurants and hotel bars encouraging everyone.

The atmosphere on the podium was more than tense. A fifth member had joined the group on the podium and he stood out in sharp contrast to the existing four. He was stocky and paled-skinned. He was also in a lively dialogue with the Minister, Xavier de la Rosa, who several times had made to stand up but been pulled back down by the new member. As the audience quietened and most started to look at the podium the fifth member thrust a mobile phone to the ear of the Minister. The Minister stood up and stepped away from the podium. He did not come back.

A member of the podium then tapped on a glass of water in front of him and he then spoke into a microphone.

"Senoras y Senores. Ladies and Gentlemen. I have an announcement to make before the shortlist. The Minister, Senor de la Rosa, has been asked by the President of the Council of Ministers, to take temporary leave from his duties. We are very sad that this has happened today. But..."

As the spokesman tried to continue there was a very lively reaction from the audience. The Minister was widely regarded as a modernising force in the Ministry and very much in favour of foreign investment. Many questions were being asked all at once. Raven and Swannel were in an animated discussion with several Australians. Trump and Dow looked perplexed. African and Arab delegates were on their feet and gesticulating. Narazov and Voronsky sat quietly. Nazarov smiled at Anna who was studying the new member on the podium. She thought she recognised his face. She was pretty certain that she had seen him leaving Zelinsky's office the last time she had been in Moscow. He might very well be part of the wider team from Moscow. She should have been glad but for some reason she was not.

"But," tried the spokesperson again this time banging his glass on the table and waiting as the audience calmed down. "But, we are very fortunate that our President has appointed an international expert to our team. Professor Ustinov here to my right is a highly experienced economic adviser who has worked on many privatisations. He has not been involved in selecting the shortlist but he will now advise the Ministry on the bidding process for the concessions although the final decision will now pass to the President of our Council of Ministers."

The audience remained quiet this time as the delegates tried to figure out what all this really meant.

Dow tapped Raven on the shoulder and said quietly, "monumetal push by the Russians! Military exercises all over the island and now advising on the tender. We need to talk and get our act together."

"Dinner is in the diary, John. Just waiting to make sure we are on the shortlist," replied Raven as he waved to the door as Kelly walked in. Kelly waved back and took a seat towards the back of the room. Whilst looking at a copy of a notice he had picked up as he had entered he scanned the room. One face stood out. The Russians were definitely here, he thought to himself. Anna looked her normal cool and collected self though Kelly did notice the rather less attractive Russian-looking males sitting next to her.

The final surprise of the press conference was welcomed by the majority of the delegates. The shortlist was not as rumoured. Of the twenty or so companies who had applied only a handful had been rejected and no one was surprised to see that the companies in question from North Africa, Laos and Bangladesh had not passed the tests of sufficient mining expertise or financial credibility. The audience now buzzed with comments on the six concessions up for auction. Most were on their feet and animated conversations in a host of languages filled the room. Only a couple of delegates noticed as a woman wearing a gown-like garment came into the room and few listened as a roll of thunder clapped overhead. The large glass windows on two sides of the room visibly darkened.

Kelly made his decision. In Tashkent he had approached Anna in public to make contact but had failed. He could see that she was talking with the Russian-looking men at the end of one of the rows of seats and next to one of the glass windows. He took the hotel leaflet for the Friday night trip and scribbled a note on it. As he stood up an almighty bang hit the conference room as a bolt of lightning flashed violently across one of the windows. The audience froze for a moment and then comments about the unpredictability of Cuban weather filled the room. Only one or two people watched as the woman in the gown left knowing that the lightning was not entirely nature's work. Kelly used the moment to cross towards Anna, stoop down at the end of a row of chairs as if to pick up something off the floor but instead he deftly placed the leaflet on top of Anna's handbag.

Anna for her part had seen Kelly arrive. As the lightning had struck she had kept her eyes on the window and watched through the reflection on the window as Kelly placed the leaflet. Several moments later she excused herself, picked up her handbag and the leaflet and made her way to the toilets. She smiled as she read the scribbled note on the leaflet: 'Licence to dance? 8pm Hotel reception.' Kelly clearly needed to talk.

Nineteen

THE Catholic church was easily recognisable by its high pink walls, pitched tiled roof, white statue on a plinth in the apex of the roof, a large cross on the roof and a large wooden front door. The building next to it was much smaller and its overall shape was similar to that of a single garage but with the side walls squeezed in a foot or so in the middle. It had a steel grilled door in two halves on the front – the outlines of the doors were like large ice cream cones. Above the door there were ornate paintings and symbols. Pieces of food and burning incense lay at the foot of the door. A temple side by side with a church. A voodoo snake house in touching distance of God's house.

Inside the church was brightly lit and an evening mass had started. The church was only a quarter full but a small and enthusiastic choir was leading the singing of an opening hymn. A priest in a white cassock with a bright purple sash draped over both his shoulders and down below his waist was walking behind three altar boys the first of whom was carrying a large cross, and the other two of whom were carrying the chalice, plate, water, wine and hosts to be used in the mass. The priest who was elderly and had largely grey hair, thick eyebrows and light blue eyes oozed calmness and devotion. Fr Omar was widely regarded as one of the most charismatic priests in Havana. He was also known as the 'compadre', the best buddy, to everyone in his 'barrio', his area. He looked after people by using whatever means he had to use.

The main action this evening in the church though was not at the mass. At one side of the altar was a small oblong room, the sacristy, where the priest and the altar boys changed. It had several cupboards and an oblong table. Three men sat at each side of the table and there was an empty chair at one end of the table. On one side sat three very local looking men – dark-skinned and widish foreheads dressed in old clothes. On the other side sat three men who looked as though they had just disembarked from a cruise ship – slightly dark-skinned but with fresh suntans and smartly dressed in polo shirts, chinos and loafers. If anyone walked in on them they could have been mistaken for being in a parish council meeting but their discussion was much more serious than that. The Exiles were uniting with their local compatriots.

Just as the six men had taken their seats, a large white van drove past the church and stopped a hundred yards on. The van was old and had been well used. To anyone passing it would just look like a delivery van parking up for the night. Inside the back of the van, however, were two men. They both wore headphones and had a number of computers and other electronic devices with them. The driver stepped out of the van, closed his door and knocked twice on the back door of the van. He was let in very discretely. The meeting now had three extra pairs of ears.

In the sacristy the Exiles were represented by a senior figure from three groups: The Friends of Cuba, the Cuba Liberation Front and the Cuban Democratic Union. The groups had distinct histories largely as a result of the backgrounds of their founders but they had gradually united over the last twenty years around three key principles – to remain strong, to lobby more and more and to wait for the Castro family to weaken. Their patience had been sorely tested every year as the longevity of the Castro family continued to astound everyone in Cuba and in America but they were sticking to the three principles and they now scented blood for the first time in fifty years.

The locals were from two groups in Havana and one group from Pinar del Rio in Western Cuba, some one hundred and twenty miles west from Havana. The local groups were less formally organised that the Exile groups and were mainly involved in the Cuban black market although some political dissidents did figure in their ranks. Most importantly they acted as brotherhoods and they knew exactly who they could and could not trust in their areas.

The discussion initially focussed on the backgrounds of the groups and their current activities. They had been called to the meeting by the self-styled leader of the nascent 'Cuba Nueva' or New Cuba movement. He was to join their 'gathering' later once the introductions had been done and several questions had been aired in an 'open' way between the uniting groups. The local seated in the middle posed the first question.

"Senors, we all have the same objective," he began, "but we here remember our history only too well."

The man opposite him nodded.

"We cannot be involved in such a dramatic fiasco again. We will never be involved in a plan like the Bay of Pigs again."

"What do you propose?" asked the man opposite slowly.

"We need funds, lots of funds. We will spread the funds directly to the people to prepare themselves and to significantly raise their standard of living. We will rise all at once across the country. Like as has happened in many countries in the last years. We will not be part of a military invasion. If we give enough people the resources they will trust us and they will follow us. We will take Cuba back without military force so that the Cuban army will come over to us and together we will defend the New Cuba. Several senior military leaders are already with us."

There was a pause. The singing of another hymn drifted into the room. The man opposite in the middle looked at both of the men at his sides in turn. He then addressed the men opposite.

"We agree with you one hundred per cent," he said softly again, "and for years we have been raising funds for such a day. Our government will also contribute."

"That is what we wanted to hear," said the local looking at the men on his side who both whispered their agreement. "We just need to find ways to bring in the funds because that is now our problem." The man explained that it had become virtually impossible to transfer any large sums into Cuba through the banking system. The regime had been succesful in controlling all banks in the country and all the various money transfer schemes had been detected.

"Can we not smuggle in cash?" asked the man opposite. "Surely those old routes for smuggling whiskey and cigarettes are still being used?"

"They were," replied the man, "and they were exactly what we had planned to use but the government has just put a stop to those as well."

"Really?" All three men opposite were genuinely surprised. This part they had expected to be the easiest. Large sums of dollars in used notes could be stored in all manner of containers, disguised and then smuggled in by sea in remote locations and via secret landing places. The coast was dotted with hidden caves and caverns and the caves and tunnels under the Hotel Nacional were such an easy route.

"The government did not mean to do this but the side effect of their military cooperation exercises with the Russians means that all the sea routes are being monitored by satellite, sonar and radar. Russian boats and submarines are everywhere around the coast."

The men opposite sat in increasing incredulity as the man went through a litany of captured boats, rafts and barrels in the previous few days. The Russians had also shown a canny knack of identifying suspected attempts to bring goods ashore. The joke in Havana was that the skills of the Russian black market operators had been used to supreme effect and that the Russians being the world's most accomplised black marketers had also spirited away all the captured goods. And how the Russians would jump at the chance of catching US-sponsored smugglers!

The Exile in the middle finally spoke. The double whammy of the banking and smuggling routes being blocked was a huge problem. Their leader was due to meet their 'friend from Virginia' after their meeting and they would have to let them discuss it further. The gathering was over but all present agreed that they were united and that the New Cuba would soon be theirs.

A moment later the door to the sacristy opened as the final line of a hymn echoed softly around. The leader had arrived. He greeted each of the six men with hugs and one with a kiss on both his cheeks. He spoke a few words to each, checking their resolve, giving them their courage. He was briefed on the issue of the problem with bringing in the quantum of funds required. He nodded sagely and smiled. 'Solutions follow problems, if one has faith or if one makes sacrifices', he said as he turned to leave. Fr Omar left the sacristy and went back into the church.

"Good to see you again, Father," said a tall man in an American accent. He was standing just inside the church at the back which was now empty. Fr Omar walked briskly to him.

"John, it is indeed a pleasure," replied Fr Omar with a smile. "We have worked so long for this moment."

Fr Omar then turned round, genuflected to the altar and made the sign of the cross whispering a short prayer of thanks. Dow followed Fr Omar and did the same.

"Yes, we have worked tirelessly. The key goups are now united and their resoltion is strong. They will now also start to show themselves in public."

"That is great news, Father," replied Dow who had gathered as much from the eavesdropping but now felt elated at the leader's confirmation.

"There is one matter, though, to address, John. They need a lot of funds and they need to have them here on the ground and spread across the island."

Dow looked at Fr Omar with a pensive look. That had been the easy part but he had heard the comments about the banks and the Russians.

"But let us pray first, John," said Fr Omar.

They prayed and then they talked. Dow then left and Fr Omar left also and closed the door to the church. Dow had understood their dilemma fully but had not replied with a solution. Fr Omar could not take any chances. He walked over to the snake house, knelt down and took out an offering. He also lit a stick of incense as he intoned an invocation of the spirits of Santeria, Cuba's voodoo religion to give it its precise name. He was joined silently be a group of women with pale faces who stood behind him and repeated his invocation very softly.

Twenty

BUNIN had called Floxly. Bunin had had some basic information back from Cuba but he felt as if he was almost in a knowledge vacuum which was something which made him nervous, very nervous.

"I see you have become active with the Cubans, Vladimir," commented Floxly after brief opening pleasanteries.

"We have taken quite a capitalistic approach and forgiven much of the old Soviet debt," replied Bunin. "You may have seen the press conference my Finance Minister gave a few days ago in Havana."

"But I am sure you will be managing to get a lot back in return," said Floxly. Bunin never did anything without seeking an advantage political or increasingly economical.

"I am hoping for some succes for one of our gold mining companies," replied Bunin, "although I suggest everyone should be wary of all figures on new deposits of gold produced by the Cubans. Sadly they followed the Soviet tendency to exaggerate for many years and old habits are hard to break."

"I hope it wont be a repeat of the Uzbek gas reserves," quipped Floxly.

"I think we have all learned from last time," replied Bunin smiling. "And this time we must not forget that the one area which is closest to Cuban hearts after such tough times created by the US and by us sadly for a time is - cash. Cash can move mountains, I believe they are whispering in Havana."

"I think it can do the same just about anywhere in the world," quipped Floxly again. This was the most open and almost frivolous conversation he had ever had with Bunin and it was beginning to unsettle him. The CIA's infamous Bay of Pigs failure was put down to the Cubans not rising up with the American insurgents because many said that the Americans brought little with them of what they had promised. The lack of cash had certainly made a huge impact. Floxly thought he would push Bunin a little. "I hear your military exercises are much more extensive than first planned."

"Has Langley been showing off its satellite pictures again?" quipped Bunin this time.

"We have some of our own sources, Vladimir, you must appreciate that."

"Of course, David, but on the ground things might be very different from how they appear from above." Bunin had tried to find a way to illicit some information from Floxly about the Americans but now he was sure that he would draw a blank. He would revert to his eyes and ears on the ground. He ended the call.

Floxly for his part was concerned that underneath such a normal conversation events were moving in Cuba. He would see what Kelly knew.

Kelly was in his hotel room when a note was pushed under his door. It simply asked him to go to the hotel's business centre where he was shown into a small booth-like room which had a telephone on a small desk and one chair. As the door was closed the phone rang. It was Floxly.

"Hello," said Kelly, "I had information from a mutual friend that calls may be difficult." He was referring to what he had been told by Floxly's PA about calls being routinely listened in to and recorded in Cuba, especially international calls.

"This line is scrambled, Jack," said Floxly warmly. "We are using satellite links and it will take the local engineers at least five minutes to track down that we are calling from somewhere in the South Pacific and a lot longer to unscramble any of our conversation. But let's be brief to be on the safe side."

"Ok," replied Kelly. "From different sources it appears that there was a reason for what happened and that that reason may be close to base." Kelly was alluding to the murder of the geologist and his suspicion of links to the company itself in some way.

"I understand," said Floxly taking the hint. "Might someone be compromised?"

"More than likely but I have not yet ruled out additional links to competitors. And even some much older European involvement in fact."

"I see. Do I need to look into this?" asked Floxly. This was a clear new line of enquiry.

"Potentially and it could involve sugar as much as gold." Kelly had been doing his best to keep his words as basic and as vague as possible and thought deeply about whether or not to use 'gold' but Floxly would have to have something to try and make the connections.

"My old job might help," said Kelly, "as might a very close client from over the pond at the time."

"That is most hopeful and what is next for you?" An American link and from Kelly's time in Moscow, thought Floxly. This again opened up interesting possibilities as much about Kelly as the present situation in Cuba.

"I hope to have a business dinner and then perhaps a sightseeing trip to the coast before coming back."

"Very good and any signs of our larger friends?" asked Floxly.

"There are movements but nothing major for now that I have seen. Contacts have been made."

"Keep on the lookout for them. Be careful of events and let me know the moment something crops up, even if you have to telephone me directly."

The call ended and Kelly sat bemused. His face flushed from the concentration. He rewound the conversation in his head. He had managed it well. His communication training had really helped him but two thoughts would not leave him.

The first was the way he had now permanently linked the 'sugar' and the 'gold'. He had to work out connection between Maria and the Spanish people he had met in Moscow and what could follow from such a connection. And then how was it linked to the dead geologist?

The second was the clear 'larger' reference to the Americans and the Russians and Floxly's comment to even risk a telephone call that would be listened in to. Did Floxly want him to be more involved? He had set up to meet Anna and he had easy access to the Americans. He would analyse as many scenarios as he could before deciding whom to say what to.

In London a senior operative from MI5 had sat in Cummings' office in the Foreign Office listening with Cummings to the call. He had tapped with great speed on a keyboard and within seconds of the call ending had sent Floxly a file. Floxly opened the file as Cummings and the operative came on the line.

"So, you think the sugar and gold references made by Kelly to his Moscow time relate to this deal?" asked Floxly as he read the file which included a press cutting from the Financial Times with the headline: 'American Agri-Giant Millingtons wins tender for Saratov Sugar Beet Collective'. Millingtons had been advised by Kelly's firm and had paid an undisclosed sum for a forty-nine per cent share in Russia's largest producer of sugar beet as the first step in its expansion into Russia. The Detroit-based private company had beaten off competiton from several large international companies including the Spanish Azucar Pena which was regarded as the biggest competitor in the tender but which had withdrawn its bid following an unrelated incident involving the company's chairman.

The paper explained in the final paragraph of the article that the chairman had been expelled from the country along with a diplomat from the Spanish Embassy. It was rumoured that the expulsions related to a private matter involving the attempted removal of maps and other valuable items from the Hermitage including ancient gold coins. The Russians had folied an 'audacious attempt to illegally repatriate items of a sensitive nature to an old Spanish family'.

"Good God!" exclaimed Floxly. "What is this all about? Sugar producers and ancient gold!"

"We will have to do more research, Prime Minister," replied the operative. "I have cross-referenced all the basic relevant information we have and these definitely look like the companies which Kelly was referring to in your conversation with him. There are no other companies anything like them in terms of the countries, products and time mentioned."

"And, David," said Cummings looking at a folder he had open on his desk. "There may be more to Kelly's link to Millingtons. The follow-up on his vetting report had a note that Kelly's uncle had several senior jobs in Detroit. And what is the betting they include Millingtons?"

"Look into everything will you, Douglas?" asked Floxly. "Let's go through it all when you exhausted all sources."

Floxly put down the phone. Kelly appeared to be far more involved in Cuba than he had anticipated and nothing had yet kicked off with either the Russians or the Americans. The thought of Americans set off a trail of recollections in Floxly's mind. Kelly had advised a major American company in Russia having turned down working for a Spanish company. He had an uncle who had become an American citizen and might be connected to this company in Detroit. Kelly and his wife had been refused access to the British Embassy when they lived in Moscow in their supposedly non-existent dacha in Barvikha outside of Moscow but they had been given passes to the US Embassy there and often spent time there. Up until now Kelly's allegiance had seemed at worst to have been some sort of fifty-fifty split between HMG and the KGB! What if Floxly was missing what was right under his nose? Did Kelly have a deeper allegiance to the Stars and Stripes at a point when the US were about to try and retake Cuba? Would Kelly hold the fate of Cuba and potentially much more in his hands? He had sent Kelly there. He sat frozen in thought.

Twenty One

THE New Cuba movement was as good as its word and it had begun to creep into Cuban life in a myriad of ways. The movement had left the cash problem to find its solution. Fr Omar was believed without question and Fr Omar in turn had to believe that the might of the US of A and its CIA would be able to materialise bundles and bundles of dollars across the island some time very soon in one way of another, though he was glad that after he had prayed to the Good Lord he had also invoked more local spirits as his back-ups. The movement was about to gain its first touch of notoriety but not of its own making.

The six groups who had met in the sacristy had agreed to make their first joint and more importantly their first public appearance. It was the feast day of Saint Anthony Mary Claret who was a Spanish missionary who had been Archbishop of Santiago de

Cuba in the mid 1800's and the groups had hatched what they thought would be a simple and uncontroversial ploy to go public.

At eleven o'clock a procession set off from the Iglesia de Santa Rita on the Quinta Avenida to walk through the wide streets of the Miramar district in honour of the saint. Several priests and children led the way. There was music played on the small three-stringed guitar called the 'tres' accompanied by the tapping on the cylindrical wooden sticks known as 'claves', the staple instruments of Cuban music. As the procession wound its way through the streets its length grew and grew as men, women and children joined the procession in groups all interlocking arms in rows of eight to ten. Any trained observer, especially from the Cuban secret police, would have noticed that the men who were joining were from the six united New Cuba groups. It was becoming their first political outing although no banners were being carried, no slogans chanted or songs sung. It was a trial run and it was being filmed by several participants to record the event and start their Internet campaign.

Kelly smiled as he watched the procession. He stood next to a very old Chevrolet. He recognised the saint from a large banner in Spanish at the front of the procession. The people all seemed very happy. He had seen religious processions in Salamanca in Spain during Semana Santa or Holy Week and he noticed the similarities. A hand of a small child grabbed at his hand as a section of the procession moved past him and the old Chevrolet. The child's face was that of a boy and for a split second the smile on the boy's face reminded Kelly of his own young boy who was nearly five years old. It was so, so full of life and such a contrast to the pale faces he had become used to seeing. As a warm feeling spread over Kelly he let the child pull him into the procession and he smiled broadly at the young woman who held the other hand of the small boy.

"Buenas tardes," said Kelly.

The young woman laughed in reply.

Less than a minute later the young woman's smile turned to pure horror and she and hundreds in the procession screamed in terror as a massive bang erupted behind them followed by another two in quick succession. Kelly instinctively grabbed the young boy and fell to the ground covering the boy's body. He then pulled at the young woman's skirt as she stood rooted to the spot her hands gripping the side of her face and shutting out the noise. The young women then also fell to the floor as Kelly pulled harder on her skirt. Kelly then lifted up his head and looked behind them.

The old Chevrolet car was ablaze. Flames were shooting out of its blackened frame and a dark plume of thick smoke was being pumped into the air through a large hole in its roof. Sirens started to sound around them as the initial screams of horror changed into moans, groans and wails. Kelly made a quick and detailed mental survey of the procession. There were people on the ground all around but Kelly was relieved to see that no one looked to have been hit by anything from the car. He calculated the distance between the car and the back of the procession. The distance was far enough – at that range the only danger would have been small flying pieces of glass and possibly of metal but he could not see any blood or injured bodies. He got up and gave the young woman who was holding onto the young boy for dear life a quick hug. She was now crying as was the young boy but they looked unhurt. Kelly started to run to the burning car but as a possee of police cars screeched to a halt around it Kelly decided to stop.

Later that evening Cuban television would show pictures of the burnt-out Chevrolet. The procession which had just passed the car had been summarily broken up by police officers for safety reasons. The incident was described as a possible bomb attack but not as yet confirmed. An investigation was underway. A loose reference to international terrorists was aired but again not elaborated on.

Back in his hotel Kelly had a stiff drink – the first offered by the barman and Kelly did not care if it was the famous Havana Club rum or not. His proximity to the bombing coupled with the frenzied actions of his bar visit and the wanton violence of the taxi ride had severely unsettled him. It felt as if he was the only person is some form of surreal all-out war in which he was being saved at the very last moment from severe violence being done to him. He was also on his own.

He did not believe for a moment that such a car bomb did not have a real and sinister reason behind it. The oblique reference on the TV to international terrorists he thought at first might be hinting at the US. It had the hallmarks of an opening shot in a CIA-sponsored black op. On the other hand could the Russians be starting a campaign of their own? A small but top-level Russian military presence was already on the island. Could they be engineering a situation which would lead to an invitation to the Russians to send in more forces? He downed a second drink. He had to look for answers from both sides. He would start with a certain Russian who would soon be arriving in the hotel's reception.

Twenty Two

ANNA's arrival soon warmed Kelly's heart more than the several stiff rums he had downed in the bar as his brain played through a list of more and more implausible explanations about what was going on. There was the violence, there were scenes of US-backed uprisings and then Russian-aided suppressions and next there was also gold. Freshly mined gold and ancient gold. Sunken ships and maps. Finally snakes and a goat. He had to relax and unwind his overloading brain. It was all revolving around gold – gold fashioned into ingots and coins and gold fresh from being mined. The trip to the Plaza Vieja would hopefully be the perfect tonic.

Anna arrived just as the dozen or so tourists boarded a hotel minibus. She was dressed in jeans and a brightly-coloured top. She had her long blond hair in a ponytail and she carried her usual handbag on which there was an extended strap so that she could carry it over her shoulder. She pecked Kelly on the cheek before climbing on board. She drew several admiring looks from the male tourists already seated on the bus. The trip was to an area of bars where 'black magic' was said to be practiced. The hotel guests were being escorted by two guides from the hotel who promised that this was authentic black magic and not a tourist 'voodoo trap' of which there were several well-known fake shows in Havana. They would also visit other bars for music and dancing.

"Great to see you, Jack," said Anna quietly as they sat down on seats at the front of the minibus.

"And you, Anna," replied Jack. His tone was a little down and Anna sensed this at once.

"Are you ok?" she asked putting her arm through his and linking them together.

"Did you hear about the car bomb this afternoon?" asked Jack a little brighter.

"Yes," replied Anna.

"I was only a few yards away and it was a miracle that no one in the procession was hurt," said Jack quietly.

Anna looked at Jack. The last time they had met they had both played their part in foiling an assassination attempt. She was hoping that her Cuban assignment would not descend into bloodshed. She would prefer some simple old-fashioned espionage or some challenging intelligence gathering although she was rarely told by her boss what was really going on at least to start with. The 'need to know' basis in the FSB seemed to translate to the latest possible moment.

"Does that have anything to do with what you are doing?" she asked.

"I don't know yet," replied Kelly. "I am here to look into an incident but it feels as though other things may be starting. And you?"

"Oh, just assisting a company as you saw at the press conference," replied Anna with a smile. "And tonight I am off duty."

"Great," replied Kelly with his first smile of the evening although neither of them believed for one moment what she had just said.

Their conversation ended as one of the hotel guides explained that they would be arriving shortly and asked that they all stick close together when moving through the streets and that if the crowds were really dense they might hold hands and form a human chain.

The minibus stopped and as the tourists descended they saw what the guide had been alluding to. The narrow streets were packed with people all of whom seemed to be locals. The air was thick with a sweet smoke mixed with an overwhelming smell of male sweat. Music pounded out of several bars. It was like a musical rave high on drugs squashed into a narrow dark tube. The female tourists all gasped while the male tourists all frowned. It was as intimidating as it was intoxicating. Kelly grabbed hold of Anna's hand tightly with one hand and took hold of a young female tourist with his other hand. The human chain set off led by one of the guides to squeeze their way through the mass of pulsating and swaying bodies.

The crowd did not part for them and they had to press forcefully to make any progress. After several minutes the front of the chain reached a bar and the guide then pulled each of them out of the crowd and into the bar. He pointed for them to go upstairs. The room upstairs was a sanctuary. It was empty and although only small it seemed to be full of space. The group visibly relaxed and readily drank the rum coxtails in coconut shells set out on a table. Kelly and Anna stood at the window and looked down on the street.

"Feels like we are in Africa," said Anna, "at some tribal gathering."

"Yes," laughed Jack, "it does seem primitive."

"Do you believe in this voodoo, Jack?" asked Anna.

"Santeria as the call their type of voodoo in Cuba? It is easy to say no, but the human mind and body can act in strange ways especially when given substances or when the mind is influenced or controlled by someone else," replied Kelly. "What do you think?"

"I agree. We have some specialists in Moscow who study it," replied Anna.

Kelly looked at her. He had not expected Anna to believe in voodoo but he had heard of the KGB department she referred to and he knew only to well that the British and above all the Americans had made many attempts to harness the darker sides of the spiritual world. The conversation was again cut short as one of the guides asked them to drink up and follow him. The crowd had eased for a moment and he had spied an opportunity to get to their main destination with less effort than before. Kelly finished his drink and Anna offered him the rest of hers.

Their main destination was remarkably similar to the bar Kelly had been in before. In a side street. In a back room. A group of locals. A throne. Thoughts of déjà vu or even the opposite mental state of clairvoyance flashed through Kelly's brain. As they sat down and took another offered drink Kelly decided to distract himself from thinking of his previous experience in the other bar and to get back on task.

"Anna, do you think your Russian mining company will be succesful?" he asked.

"I am sure it will be," replied Anna, "we have lots of resources."

The second comment jolted Kelly. Maybe the Russians were interested in more than a mining project in Cuba and, of course, why have Anna and the FSB involved.

"I have been dealing with a similar British company," replied Kelly.

This time it was Anna's turn to be surprised though she did not show it.

"London asked me to find out why its top geologist was murdered here in Havana," continued Kelly.

"And have you?" asked Anna.

"I have some possible explanations," replied Kelly deciding that it was time to try and see if there was any potential link to the Russians. "The most likely scenario is that someone was after his work," he paused and looked directly at Anna, "his latest work on the location of gold deposits."

Anna held Kelly's gaze. She understood where he was coming from and she had to admit that such an act was the kind which her colleagues at Cyprus Gold would happily commit without blinking an eye but she had not heard anything about the murder.

"Such information could be valuable to many companies. Especially if there were new maps," she replied just slowly enough for Kelly to realise that she was not ruling out anyone including the Russians but neither was she admitting that it was. Anna herself then thought back to a comment her boss had made to her when he had briefed her before she had set off Cuba. He had mentioned the unexplained murder of a museum curator of ancient maps in Moscow. The curator's speciality had been Latin America including Cuba and an old map had gone missing. "Maps can be extremely valuable," she continued. "We also have an unusual murder case which we are investigating in Moscow."

"Really?" asked Kelly his mind clicking into gear despite the build up of alcohol in his system.

"The map in Moscow is also of Cuba, though, it is an ancient map," she said with a slight shrug of her shoulder.

Jack's analytical training kicked in. Finding the link. The less than obvious but underlying link. You need to put combinations together and sometimes the most unlikely items, people or places will match. His brain though was slowing and as it started to numb the chanting in the room started.

The tourists looked on horrified as a woman and man dressed in red robes came in and sat on the throne. Kelly looked frantically around the altar. No box. That was a relief. The man stood up and spoke to the crowd. He held a small dagger and although his voice was stern it was nothing like the rant the man in the other bar had made. The woman then went to the corner of the room where there was a basket covered in a large red silk cloth. She came back to the throne carrying a chicken which had a red ribbon around its neck. Jack had not seen what had finally happened to the goat and the girl in the previous ritual but it did not take too much imagination to fear the worst.

As the tourists stared at the spectacle they were offered another drink which most including Kelly accepted. A light almost white smoke was swirling around the throne as the woman held up the chicken and started a chant of her own. The man also stood up and started to sway side by side raising and then lowering his dagger. Jack looked quickly at their group. The guides sat with passive looks on their faces, some of the female tourists looked as they were about to faint.

The people around them started to chant and to stand. Clapping also started.

Kelly took a quick glance at Anna who had one of her hands now in her handbag as the smoke intensified and swirled around the woman and the chicken. The woman was also now spinning around. She lifted the chicken by its feet above her head and the man lifted the dagger as high as he could and with a bloodcurdling shout he froze as if he had leapt off the ground. The woman screamed and fell to the floor in a heap. The chicken had vanished. The man sat back down on his throne. The room fell silent and then the guides applauded. The tourists slumped in their seats and the locals began to talk and clap. Before they left the bar to move on to some music and dancing the guides explained that the spiriting away of a chicken was an old Santeria way of warding off evil spirits. They would now have a much more relaxing part of their evening trip.

Kelly and Anna mingled with the other hotel guests in the music bar. The music was a mix of salsa, son and ramba played on tradional guitars, drums and various maracas. All the hotel guests had recovered from what they had witnessed and they all agreed that there had been nothing touristy about any of it. They all though had had several quick drinks as soon as they had arrived in the music bar. Kelly was savouring his third double Havana Club rum whilst Anna had moved onto to a second cocktail. Before long most of the hotel guests were dancing and even Kelly took the plunge. Anna had not needed a second request from one of the male tourists and was dancing enthusiastically if a little rigid in her movements.

After a couple of songs Kelly moved to the door of the bar looking to get some fresh air but he was disappointed. The smoke, which he knew came from a strong strain of marijuana, still filled the streets like a fog. Without thinking he took a deep breath and his lungs filled. He exhaled slowly and closed his eyes slightly as he reran in his mind the disappearing of the chicken. This time the chicken was replaced and replaced by a shower of shining objects. Gold. Gold. His befuddled brain was making a connection. It was time to share what he thought with Anna.

The music bar was on a narrow road but the occasional car passed the bar. As Anna came to join him, Kelly caught the sight of a taxi coming towards the bar. Its lights flashed in short bursts. The driver was signalling to someone.

"Have you stopped dancing, Jack?" asked Anna as she unclipped the clip on her ponytail and let her long blonde hair fall around her shoulders.

"I was just looking to get some air," replied Kelly, "and perhaps have a quick chat."

"By all means," said Anna shaking her long hair and then lifting it off her neck. "What's on your mind?"

"You might think this crazy, Anna, but I have a feeling that there is more than one source or rather type of gold on the island."

Anna put her hairclip into her handbag and was about to reply that there were at least six deposits assuming the data given on the six concessions had not been falsified when the taxi stopped abruptly next to them and its passenger door opened. Kelly grabbed Anna's hand and jumped into the taxi pulling her with him.

"Jack!" shouted Anna. "What do you think you are doing?"

Before Kelly could reply the tyres on the taxi screeched violently as the driver set off.

"I don't know," replied Kelly looking frantically to the road ahead. "Just do as I say!"

And as he said that a baseball bat shattered the windscreen of the taxi which shuddered to an abrupt halt.

"Move over, Anna," yelled Jack as his passenger door was pulled open. As the scantily-dressed young woman jumped in Kelly pushed her down and made her lie under his and Anna's feet.

"Reverse," shouted Kelly at the taxi driver with such force and power that the taxi driver yanked the taxi into reverse as quickly as he could. As the taxi driver concentrated on looking into his rear-view mirror, Kelly stared ahead. The truck was coming straight forwards at them and speeding up. Anna had taken out her handgun and pointed it at Kelly.

"What the hell are you doing?" she asked wiping her dishevelled hair from her face.

"Just a few moments and we will be ok," replied Kelly as he lent forward and grapped the sterring wheel from the driver. "Brake hard," he shouted as he swung the streering wheel violently ninety degrees to the left. The taxi almost went up on its side as it shot into a side street and then banged its tyres on the road. The truck flew passed at an amazing speed.

"Get up," said Kelly to the young woman again in a commanding voice. "Get out and find somewhere safe," he contiuned as he manhandled her out onto the street. "Drive straight across," he ordered the driver this time in a calmer voice. He had to find the gate.

"Jack, if you do not tell me what the hell you are doing, I am going to shoot you," said Anna her voice trembling as she pushed her handgun into Kelly's thigh.

"Turn at that gate," ordered Kelly as the taxi had entered the side street opposite and he spied a gate on the left. "Anna," he said quietly. "Bear with me. This is a deja vu but in reverse. I have seen what is happening."

"What? This clairvoyance nonsense? Have you drunk too much?"

"We are going to have to act fast," said Kelly again calmly as the gate opened before them and the taxi drove into a courtyard. Kelly scanned the scene. It was the opium den from hell again. Needles were everywhere, a thick smoke was rising and bodies sitting and laying on the ground were moaning as much as in pain as in pleasure. All the faces were deathly pale. Kelly motioned for them both to get out of the taxi.

"Just shoot the whip, Anna," he said to Anna. He then turned and spoke to the driver. "You take the man they will chase and drive as far away as you can." Kelly put a roll of dollar bills into the pocket of the taxi driver's shirt.

"Anna, over here," said Kelly as he crouched down behind a small wall a few yards in front of the taxi. As soon as Anna crouched down next to Kelly there was the thundering sound of the cracking of a whip. Into the courtyard ran a man frantically looking for somewhere to run. His eyes locked onto Kelly's but this time Kelly looked back at him calmly and Kelly pointed to the taxi. But as the man took his next step a swarm of armed men surrounded him out of nowhere. The man with the whip also materialised complete with a large swirl of white smoke. Anna aimed her gun at him.

"Wait," said Kelly, "I'll tell you when to shoot the whip."

Anna looked on in complete horror as the whip was flicked around the man's neck and he was hoisted in the air as the whip snarled around the branch of an overhanging tree. Kelly had gripped Anna's arm.

"Now," he whispered.

Anna fired and the whip snapped into two with an immediate and loud shout of total surprise filling the air.

"Run," said Kelly as he grabbed Anna and set off back past the taxi. The man had landed on his feet and with a dozen giant steps had reached the taxi. The man with the whip had been sent flying backwards as his whip had been shot in two. That gave Kelly and Anna the few precious seconds they needed to exit the courtyard before the gang could follow them. They ran through the gate and kept running as fast as they could. The chase was on.

"Where to?" panted Anna.

"The hotel minibus," replied Jack breathing very heavily.

They ran for their lives and looked in horror as they rounded the corner to the street where their evening had begun to see the hotel minibus moving slowly in the opposite direction. Anna stopped and aimed her handgun at the minibus. She had decided that it was going nowhere without them. Kelly knocked her arm and then wrestled her to the side of the street.

In a split second Kelly had seen the minibus stop. It was now reversing and one of the guides had his head out of the window and was waving to them. Kelly grabbed Anna in a full embrace such that it would look to the minibus as they were having a moment of romantic passion. He then span around and pulled her with him towards the minibus which was cheering them on. Once they had boarded the minibus to a round of raucous comments Kelly looked through the back of the window. A man had come round the corner. He had a small whip and he was using it to hurry a half a dozen chickens down the street.

Twenty Three

THE New Cuba movement had a star guest at its next gathering. The private room this time was at the back of a restaurant near the Cathedral of San Cristobal. It was used for poker games and its location was known only to a very elite few of Havana's wealthy gamblers. The same six men sat either side of the long oblong table. This time they were not sat as two separate groups; they had mixed Exiles with Cubans.

Fr Omar as leader of the movement sat at the head of the table and opposite him at the other end sat a well-dressed man – Xavier de la Rosa, the suspended Minister for Energy and Mines. Coffee had been served by the restaurant owner in person. No one dining or working in the restaurant would know of the presence of the group. They were not eating as it would have been impossible to serve and then spirit away eight meals in such a well-run establishment.

De la Rosa had given a brief but highly encouraging vision for the New Cuba. Elections would be held as soon as the uprising was complete and once the Armed Forces and the police had sworn their allegiances to the New Cuba. De la Rosa knew several key figures in both the military and the police and he had been instrumental in approaching and converting them to their cause.

"So, do you think that your suspension as Minister by the President is because you are suspected of these matters?" asked Fr Omar.

There were murmurs of consternation around the table.

"No," replied de la Rosa with a smile. "My suspension was engineered precisely to create a smokescreen."

"How so?" asked one of the men, the other men leaning forward to listen.

"The President was informed by several sources including our friends in the secret police that I was becoming too friendly with international companies who might not share the President's plans for our mining industry. I might fix the tenders so that anti-Cuban companies and the countries behind them won. And if this happened in the gold mining concessions then it might infect other areas," said de la Rosa with a polished smile. "They suspect me also of a financial motive and I know that I am not on any lists of suspected Exile sympathisers."

"This is truly well planned, Xavier," said Fr Omar. "You will have a very actve role to play in the New Cuba but you know that we must all stay hidden as long as possible."

Everyone agreed. Fr Omar then turned to the one question everyone wanted to ask.

"Our other friends," said Fr Omar with a composed look on his face, "are considering several alternatives on how to transport all the funds to us here on the ground. And before you ask, I have given them a target date but this date I must keep secret for now." He paused and then continued, "we have waited more than fifty years and it should not hurt us to wait a few weeks more."

The word 'weeks' electrified the room. Animated discussions broke out in pairs. There was so much to do. They could see and hear what would happen. It took Fr Omar nearly ten minutes to bring the discussion to order and to thank de la Rosa for coming. De la Rosa said he would leave first and Fr Omar said that he would follow him out shortly.

De la Rosa declined to climb the wire fence next to the rubbish bins at the back of the restaurant. He joked that he had never thought in his wildest dreams that he would have to act like a guerrilla fighter. The restaurant owner suggested that he take a quick coffee at the bar before leaving out of the front of the restauarnt so as not to raise any suspicions. De la Rosa thought it a more appropriate plan. Fr Omar joined a table of religious clergy dining in the restaurant for a brief chat before leaving the restaurant closely after de la Rosa.

It was a warm day. De la Rosa stepped onto the pavement and signalled to a taxi parked fifty yards away. Suspension meant no official car. As the taxi drove towards him a motorbike with a motorcyclist in a blacked-out helmet and visor sped past the taxi. Fr Omar stopped in the doorway of the restaurant. He looked quickly at the motorcyclist, at de la Rosa and at a man across the street dressed in a dark gown which looked like a priest's cassock. The man immediately nodded at Fr Omar in recognition. Before Fr Omar could act any further the motorbike stopped a few feet away from de la Rosa, the motorcyclist raised a pistol, shot de la Rosa three times and then paused.

Movement on the street had frozen. It was not busy but the sounds of the shots had stopped everyone moving. The motorcyclist fired one more shot in the lifeless body of de la Rosa as dark blood began to seep from underneath the prostrate body. The motorcyclist then put the pistol in his jacket pocket and pulled out an object which he threw towards the body. The object fluttered for a second and then landed close to de la Rosa's outstreched but motionless hand.

Fr Omar finally reacted. He pointed at the man in the dark gown and then at the motorcyclist. Immediately and as if on cue the man pulled a rod out of his gown. He shouted at the sky and then pointed the rod at the motorcyclist. The motorcyclist ignored the man, throttled his engine and set off. His front wheel reared up as he revved again and he sped off doing a wheelie. The front wheel of the motorbike then crashed onto the road and the motorbike instead of zooming off seemed to stop in the air. As this happened the motorcyclist jumped off and then threw himself on the ground writhing in agony. Fr Omar was shouting at all the onlookers to go inside which most did immediately.

The shooting was the leading report on Cuban TV that evening. De la Rosa was praised extensively for 'his tireless efforts and tremendous energy as a Minister' and it was announced that earlier that day the President had decided to reinstate him but sadly, as it had transpired, not in time. No one though really cared if this was true or political expediency by the President. New Cuba would have a great martyr but Fr Omar had issued his first written order forbidding anyone to mention this yet.

If this got out of hand and they were pushed into an unprepared uprising with no funds then all would be lost. The order was enforced with heavy discipline.

And to further draw attention away from de la Rosa and New Cuba, stories were whispered about the awesome power of Santeria, the Cuban voodoo. The assassin had paid with his own life and suffered a most horrendous death, a death ten times more painful than the pain of death by a simple shooting as befits anyone who does evil to others. He had torn his own clothes off and bitten his own flesh until with a trembling hand he had shot himself in the groin and then in the stomach before the police could stop him. Another rumour also spread quickly. The assassin had left a calling card – a postcard from Cyprus. Many quickly put two and two together and whispered, 'the Russians'.

Twenty Four

FOLLOWING a call from a flustered Gifford, Kelly had confirmed that he would be delighted to join Newgold for dinner as previously invited. The dinner Gifford had explained was with the Canadian company, CCMC, to explore potential areas of cooperation now that both compannies were on the shortlist and it was to be held at the appartment of a Canadian Embassy official. Kelly had thanked Gifford and said he would make his own way there.

The appartment was very similar to the one rented by Gifford. Kelly was warmly welcomed by Raven and Swannell and introduced to Bill Trump and John Dow from CCMC. Kelly was delighted to see that Maria, Gifford's wife, was there. She and the Canadian Embassy official's wife were the only two women present. Maria was helping the other woman with the meal and Maria greeted Kelly with kisses on both cheeks. Kelly felt as though he had known Maria and Gifford for years such was their open display of familiarity towards him. Gifford also surprised Kelly such was the bonhomie he was generating between all present. His slightly dishevelled look belied the obvious diplomatic skills he was now showing as he guided the discussion between Raven and Trump to the point where cooperation sounded a fait accompli and he dropped out of the conversation. Gifford then turned to Kelly.

"How is the paperwork, Jack?" he asked.

"Pretty much done, thanks, Gifford," replied Kelly, "and I will be heading home in a few days."

"Surely you must have some time for sightseeing, Jack?" said Maria as she sat down opposite him and next to Dow. Gifford was at the head of the long oval table at one end and his Canadian counterpart was at the other.

"I might have a couple of days free before going back. Where would you recommend?" replied Kelly who then sat back and listened to Maria. Her speech was captivating. Her Spanish accent alluring. Jack could not take his eyes off her and felt as though that was exactly what was expected of him. He felt himself relaxing and relaxing a bit too much. After the night out in the Plaza Vieja he thought that he deserved some normality.

Finally a comment from Trump jolted him out of his comfort zone.

"Have the police come up with anything about what happened to your geologist, Malcolm?" he asked. Everyone else paused and looked at Raven.

"Nothing, I"m afraid, Bill," replied Raven.

"Well, to be on the safe side we have doubled security all round."

"Probably wise, although, a simple robbery looks like the probable motive."

With that the other conversations resumed. Kelly's mind though reverted to his task as Maria stood up and helped the hostess to collect in plates. Robbery, but why? He thought to himself. Why say that now? Raven had said that all the geologist's work was in his office and yet even the press had mentioned the geologist's latest work on the location of deposits could most likely have been taken. Newgold's story was not consistent.

Kelly then made a mental summary of what he knew from his first contact with Anna. An ancient map of Cuba stolen in Moscow recently. More than likely La Carta del Oro Oculto, or one of the copies of it. Clearly the Russians were onto things and he was pretty sure that Anna would be working it out shortly. The

Americans. He had to use his opportunity to see what he could find about about them or better still from them.

Although CCMC and Trump were Canadian and most likely genuine, John Dow to Kelly was pure CIA. Kelly's specialist language training had focussed on the accents you had to recognise and a CIA accent was up there with the Russian accents at the top of the list. They were taking a break and Kelly spotted his chance. Trump was shepherding Raven and Swannell back into the sitting room, Gifford was talking with his Canadian counterpart and that just left Dow and him. Luckily Dow had taken out a cigarette.

"I guess," said Kelly casually, "they might prefer if we smoked on a balcony."

"Of course," replied Dow. "Care to join me?"

Kelly nodded. He did not smoke so he would make an excuse. They moved to the balcony. The balcony had an iron railing and could accommodate two to three people. The balcony looked down into a square internal garden and patio below.

"I would love to, John," said Kelly pretending to look eagerly at the cigarette Dow was offering. "I'm down to one a day. At breakfast."

"A man with strong self-control," laughed Dow. "You Brits sure surprise me sometimes." He took a drag on his cigarette and leaned over the balcony resting his forearms on the rails.

"And what brings an American to Cuba?" asked Kelly smiling at Dow.

"Surprise number two," said Dow with just the slightest hint of hostility in his voice. He stared at Kelly and then laughed again.

"Your teams have never prospered well here, at least since Castro," continued Kelly. He was pushing it, he knew.

"My, my," replied Dow flicking the butt of his still lit cigarette into the garden. "MI6, I presume?"

"Let's just say we have worked together in the past. Not personally of course," said Kelly with a smile. "And I have family in the US who have done their service for Uncle Sam."

Dow put out his hand and Kelly shook it. Down below in the bushes of the garden a camera whirred into action.

"But this time I hope you will understand that I am off the grid," replied Dow. "A very unique situation which may bring about a major change."

"I am only interested in finding out about the death of our geologist, John," said Kelly.

Dow nodded. "But it is good to know," continued Dow who was speaking now with an assured authority in his voice, "that you are on the island." Dow took a card from his pocket and handed it to Kelly. Again the camera down below whirred. "That's where you can get me if you need any help. Your geologist might not be the last. You need to watch out for yourself."

"Ah, there you two are!" boomed Gifford stepping onto the balcony. "What a wonderful evening. Cheese and port?"

The dinner resumed. Kelly was pleased with himself. Dow had been remarkably straightforward. Too straightforward though. Kelly had acted well. Dow had wanted to put Kelly off his scent and the offer of helping him with an attached veiled threat was pure Langley. Dow was clearly at the top of his game and Kelly mulled over the hint of 'a major change' which he was sure meant an event in the US favour - but how?

"Gifford," said Kelly thinking of how he might open up the conversation a little. "Did you not say that you had run into some bad sorts in Miami recently?"

"Yes, I was almost mugged. I was threatened but luckily the mugging-to-be was disturbed and they ran off!" he replied.

"Miami can be a violent and dangerous place in some parts," said Dow before contuinuing in a Mickey Mouse voice. "Disney World excepted, of course!"

Everyone laughed. Dow stood up and excused himself citing the need for a comfort break.

"Yes," said Gifford. "Now that I think about it, Jack, there was a gruesome murder. I read about it because it was near the Freedom Tower which was the building, you know, which the Americans used to check all the people who fled from Cuba. I have kept the newspaper if you think it might be useful. A witness thought that they had seen the man murdered for something in a long tube. A picture or a painting perhaps."

Kelly's mind blurred. In his exprience long tubes were used to carry one item only. In Russia certainly they had always been used for such an item especially when related to oil and metals. Pictures and paintings were better in large oblong-shaped portfolio cases. This was a connection of all connections. Kelly knew the man had been murdered for just such an item. For a map.

"I'd like to read the newspaper," said Kelly.

"It is in my briefcase so I'll get it before you go," replied Gifford. "Now let me see what kind of good malt whiskies our Canadian hosts have. Can't be doing with all this rum."

The diners chatted and drank for another hour. Gifford's challenges with money was the butt of most of the jokes with his wife taking umbrage in a very Mediterranean way about her being the root and cause of Clifford's financial challenges. She had a very healthy allowance from her family which she was tired of explaining to everyone and frankly she just did not know what Gifford did with their money!

Raven and Swanell then said that they had better leave as they had a lot to work on in the morning. They offered the others a lift which Trump accepted immediately. It was a clear sign to everyone that a deal was being hatched by the three. Kelly said that he would enjoy the stroll to his hotel. Dow said similar and Gifford and Maria said they would stay a bit longer before calling a taxi.

Kelly went to the bathroom. The window was open and it was now a cool evening. Kelly took a deep breath and inhaled. A pungent aroma knocked him for six. He looked out of the window and caught a flash from something in the bushes below. The window was not very big. He left the bathroon and entered the next room. It was the master bedroom. He walked to the balcony behind the curtains which hung from the ceiling to the floor and stepped out onto the balcony being careful to stay hidden in a shadow. The aroma had been the perfume 'Opium' by Yves St Laurent. She had not worn it the night of the trip to the Plaza Vieja. He scanned the garden and then froze. There were people now in the master bedroom.

With very slow movements he turned around and peeped into a gap in the curtains. Maria and Dow were in an embrace. Kelly had to stop himself from reacting. He closed his eyes for a second and then concentrated with all his strength. He listened.

"Soon, soon, my love," said Maria as hers and Dow's mouths interlocked, their kissing intense. "Soon, my family's wealth will be restored and we will live together in the luxury we so both deserve."

"We will, we will," said Dow breathing heavily as he twirled her round and pushed his body into her. She moaned and Dow had to put his hand over her mouth. At the sound of footsteps the embrace was broken and in a flash Maria was at the door. She opened it and stepped quickly out not looking behind herself. A few seconds later Dow did the same and quickly after that so did Kelly.

Kelly thanked the Canadians for the dinner as the final goodbyes were made. Gifford handed Kelly the newspaper as he was leaving and said quietly that the follow-up dinner would be at his place in a couple of days' time. Kelly said in all honesty that he could not wait. He now just had to find out why Anna had been watching and work out what this third murder in Miami, this 'murder for a map' as he was convinced it was, was all about. The most likely suspect of a murder in Miami would be an American and, if it were, it would no doubt lead back some way or another to the CIA.

Twenty Five

THE Russians had transformed a section of their basement room. They had erected a small tent with a metal table inside and a dehumidifier was humming away inside the tent. A large lamp on the table threw off a strong beam of light onto the table top in the otherwise dim light. It looked like a makeshift operating theatre. Nazarov was dressed in a surgeon's gown complete with mask and gloves. Varonsky passed a metal case through the door flap of the tent and then zipped the flap up. Automatically he stood in front of the tent and took out his gun. He had been told to stand guard.

Nazarov set to work. He had a second case, a steel briefcase. Its locks had been drilled and he opened the case and took out a raft of papers which he filtered through until he found what he was looking for. It was a draft geological map. The outline was that of the Western half of Cuba and three areas had markings and notes on them. On one of the areas there was a large circle, some geographical coordinates and a question mark. He flatened the map on the table.

He then turned to the metal case and opened it slowly. As he did a small puff of dust rose up, the dust particles dancing in the light of the lamp. He waited till the dust settled and then with a slightly shaking hand picked up a scroll from inside he case. He undid the ribbon around the scroll and delicately unrolled the scroll. The parchment creaked as he did so and tiny cracks appeared. It was also a map. An ancient handdrawn map of part of an island with an elaborate compass in one corner. He placed the ancient map next to the first map but did not flatten it. His eyes flitted from one map to the other showing a deep concentration and then he swore, swore and swore.

Five minutes later he had packed up both maps, switched off the lamp and dehumifier and taken off his gown, mask and gloves. Varonsky had heard the muffled swearing and just looked questioningly at Nazarov.

"Get Zelinsky on the phone, Pavel," said Nazarov.

"But boss, he said not to use the phone," objected Varonsky.

"It will be quick," replied Nazarov.

At the mention of 'Zelinsky' Anna's head shot up and she almost banged her head on the inside of the cupboard under the sink where she was hiding. She had been there for more than an hour and had fought off attacks of cramp several times. Over the last twenty-four hours she had been watching her so-called colleagues very carefully and when she had overheard them agree at breakfast when to come to the basement she had made her way there ten minutes before and chosen her hiding place after taking pictures of the tent.

Varonsky gave Nazarov his mobile and Nazarov began to pace around the basement. There was a brief argument at the beginning of the call and then Nazarov spoke quietly into the phone.

"Yes, you can report to Vlad that we have agreed a deal for the nickel, if you want, but we have a difficulty." Nararov stopped. As Anna waited for him to speak again she made a note of the comment. She assumed by 'Vlad' Nazarov meant the President. Never in a million years would she had expected anyone to speak about the President in such a casual and informal manner.

"We do not have a match yet. The data is not complete," continued Nazarov and then stopping again. This time Anna could almost hear the vent of anger from the other person on the phone. Nazarov then ended the call and three seconds later a message pinged on the phone.

"What did he say, boss?" asked Varonsky.

"Never mind, Pavel. It was what you would expect," replied Nazarov looking at the screen on the phone and then whistling softly. "One thing is ok, though, Pavel," continued Nazarov, "he says that he has been told that the doubloons will be worth an average price of just over $12,000 each when we find them. The Chinese will buy the lot. Just work out how much the 90,000 gold doubloons are now worth?"

"But you said that these Charles II gold coins could be worth $15,000 to $20,000 each," replied Varonsky puzzled.

"Yes, but such a price would be if there were only a few hundred or so of them found. We want to sell all 90,000 as quick as we can."

"Oh," replied Varonsky not understanding.

"Just work out how much we will get," said Nazarov with a huge smile.

Anna's mental arithmetic was far quicker than Varonsky's as in the blink of an eye she calculated the value to be more than a billion dollars, one billion and eighty million dollars to be precise. It would take an enormous amount of newly mined gold to reach that value. At forty dollars a kilo it would mean over twenty five thousand tonnes of new gold. No wonder they were more interested in finding these ancient gold coins, or doubloons as Nazarov had called them, rather than winning new gold mining concessions!

She was further surprised that afternoon when she met with Nazarov in the hotel to discuss the gold tender and asked in all innocence if Cyprus Gold was interested in any other metal in Cuba, nickel perhaps and Nazarov just shook his head and said not at all. FSB current, former or not, who on earth would risk lying to her President and no matter how much money was involved?

Twenty Six

THE follow-up dinner at the Gifford's appartment followed a similar formula to the dinner at the Canadian diplomat's appartment except that the seating plan was subtly changed by Gifford such that Raven, Swannell and Trump were at one end, the diplomats and their wives in the middle and Dow and Kelly at the other end. Whilst one end of the table had a piece of paper and pen and were drafting various notes in hushed whispers, at the other end Dow was steering his conversation with Kelly onto Kelly's family in the States whilst in the middle the diplomats stuck to gossip and rumours about events on the island. Alongside the interest raised by the gold tender, the main topics of gossip surrounded the shooting of de la Rosa, rumours of a new movement to free Cuba and the Russian-Cuban military exercises which were catching smugglers by the bucketfull. The world had started to watch events in Cuba very carefully. The main embassies in Havana were being bombarded with requests by their home countries for information on events and newsreporters were flying in by the day.

Raven led the cooperation discussion with Trump as Swannell made notes. Such cooperations were expressly forbidden in the tender which only allowed single bidders who would then own 49 per cent of a concession with the Cuban government holding the 51 per cent balance. The foreign company would dig and then operate the mine with the Cuban government having a say in the sales of the mined gold. Raven and Trump were running through different ways of circumventing this minor legal obstacle as they saw it. There were two broad thrusts.

The first was to set up a subsidiary for a concession and then let the other company own part of it in an offshore stucture which the Cubans would not be able to find. The second was to hire the other company's assets or services once a concession was won. In either route Newgold and CCMC had agreed that they wanted to win control of three of the concessions which they firmly believed would be the most lucrative by far. The main fears of competing bids were from companies from Australia and Saudi Arabia and now also the Russians at Cyprus Gold after the appointment of the Russian adviser to the tender.

Kelly and Dow listened occasionally to fragments of the conversation at the other end of the table and Dow at one stage was summoned over to Trump for a brief tete-a-tete. Dow, though, was probing Kelly.

"I undertand that your uncle is also a 'Kelly'," he said with the slightest twinkle in his eye.

"Was," replied Kelly feigning a touch of sadness.

"My condolences," said Dow with a short nod. "I understood that he had retired from Millingtons."

At the name 'Millingtons' Kelly could have froze but he shot back without hesitation. "Briefly, after he retired from General Motors, yes. He was a HR consultant. He had deep experience in downsizing personnel at General Motors which Millingtons paid him handsomely for."

"Very interesting, Jack. Was he always in HR?"

"Pretty much as I remember," replied Jack.

The conversation continued but Kelly gave few other details and managed to turn the conversation round so that he could work out what Dow had found out. There was a clearly a file on his uncle somewhere and most likely at Langley which Dow had probably accessed. Dow was runnning through a potted corporate history of Millingtons when Maria returned to the table carrying the last two plates of dessert which were for Kelly and herself. This time the name of 'Millingtons' made her stop and almost drop a crème brule into Kelly's lap. As she sat down next to Kelly she swore under her breath in Spanish and then apologised to Kelly for nearly dropping his dessert.

"Don't worry, Maria," replied Kelly, "y me llaman peor qu'esso en Madrid," he whispred to her in Spanish ('and they call me much worse than that in Madrid'). She blushed and threw a dagger of a look of anger at Dow.

"Maria, you seem angry," said Dow who had missed the exchange in Spanish. "Are you ok?"

"All this talk of big companies makes me sad," she replied. She looked briefly at Kelly who avoided her look and studied his crème brule somewhat overintently before delving in with his dessert spoon.

"Oh, because of what your family lost?" said Dow.

Maria did not reply and like Kelly started to eat her dessert. Kelly marvelled at the delicacy of the way she used her dessert spoon and of the sensual way she put the spoon to her mouth.

"It was a shame that lightning should strike your family twice in such a devastating way," said Dow. Kelly was not sure what Dow was trying to do. He had seen the passion with which the pair had embraced. They were clearly involved and yet Dow seemed to revel in teasing her.

"Did you know, Jack, that the de la Pena family lost its gold concessions in Peru in the eighteenth century and then its sugar plantations on Cuba in the 1960's? Massive losses."

"I saw the portrait in the sitting room of Xavier de la Pena," replied Jack finissing a mouthful. "And I met a sugar company from Spain when I worked in Moscow."

"Well, I just hope that one day the family's fortunes may change," said Dow with a knowing look at Maria at which point Trump motioned for Dow to join him at the other end of the table. Dow excused himself.

A connection about the long lost gold and Dow suddenly pinged in Kelly's brain but before he could think any further he felt a hand on his knee and he turned to look at Maria who with her eyes signaled for him to follow her as she picked up his dessert plate and hers, stood up and left the room. Kelly caught Gifford's eye. Gifford had been in a lively debate with his Canadian counterpart before they were both brought into the cooperation discussion. Kelly mouthed that he needed a short comfort break and Gifford nodded back briskly.

Maria was standing in the doorway of the kitchen and as Kelly aproached she pointed to the corridor and within seconds they were in the main bedroom. Maria locked the door behind them and approached Kelly. She slowly put her arms around his waist. She looked him powerfully in the eyes.

"So you have worked out my Spanish family connections, Jack. The gold and the sugar?" Maria pulled him closer. Her eyes were now on fire. "But, of course, you were an MI6 officer or similar then in Moscow, weren't you? MI6, FSB, CIA? They are all the same to me," she said.

She had spoken the words a little too loudly for Kelly's liking. He prided himself on never being referred to as such or even mentioned in the same sentence as any of those names. In all his time in Moscow such utterances were taboo. It kept the mystique and it was the best form of protection. All sides thought you obviously worked for one agency or another. The etiquette was to never challenge and never to reveal. Before Maria could open her mouth to speak again he kissed her strongly. Despite Maria smoking, her mouth tasted of pure honey.

Maria responded simultaneously. As the kiss intensified and Maria's body seemed to melt Kelly opened one eye. He looked over her shoulder and froze.

Maria's body shuddered and she broke the embrace. Kelly's eyes had lighted upon a large jewellery box with the crest of a pile of gold coins surrounded by a snake. Maria turned, picked up the jewellery box and then turned back round and sat at the edge of the bed. Kelly was still standing.

"So, Senor Kelly," said Maria her accent becoming more Spanish, "it would seem as though rather than just kiss you would prefer to take a look." Maria shuffled further on to the bed and with the flirting look of heaving desire she undid a button on her blouse and in the voice of an accomplished seductress whispered, "inside the chest." At which point she opened the jewellery box to reveal a rolled-up parchment. "Now maybe we can talk real business while the others finish their plan to conspire to beat the Russians?"

The next five minutes changed Kelly's mind about Maria completely. He now knew exactly what was at stake and he could but wonder at the monumental value that was so close and ready for the taking. What he still had to work out though was who was after it and why, although he knew he was pretty close to the answers.

Twenty Seven

DE la Rosa's shooting had an unintended consequence. A fierce debate had broken out over the timing and the format of his funeral. His body had been on display in an open casket in the Church of Santa Rita for two days and his family wanted him to be buried but the authorities appeared to want to delay the burial even though the shooting was an open and shut case. All attention was now focussed on identifying the assassin who had so publicly commited suicide and finding the assassin's accomplices. As a demonstration of family and friends began outside the Town Hall, the New Cuba movement spied its chance – the funeral would be followed by rallies. What easier way to get people onto the streets and not just in Havana.

Cuba's secret police, the Seguridad del Estado, or the SDE for short, to give them their proper name, though had historically been well trained and were still very capable of finding out what people might be planning. Stasi agents from the former East Germany had trained and organised the SDE for many years in the 1970's and 1980's. The SDE also had a team from Russia's FSB currently working with them as part of the military cooperation excercises between Cuba and Russia. The President and his brother though had not ruled Cuba since 1959 without learning how their so-called international friends could turn on them when it suited them. The FSB presence had been initially accepted though resistance from some SDE operatives was becoming noticeable. After a briefing on the funeral from the SDE the President started to act.

De la Rosa's body was given back to the family before the crowd gathering outside the Town Hall became too large. The crowd dispersed quickly without complaint and preparations for the funeral went into top speed. The New Cuba movement had little time to organise especially as phone calls could not be made for fear of being listened to and so runners were sent out to all the barrios on the route of the funeral procession to urge all citizens to join the procession. Church services in honour of the deceased were hastily planned in several other key cities with the idea floated for small processions around church squares after the services.

As word of these preparations was conveyed back to the President by SDE officers, cancelling the funeral procession and ordering a private burial for family only was considered. The President decided otherwise. At 9 pm that evening the President went on national TV to give his condolences to the de la Rosa family and to wish the family a dignified funeral. The President continued by hoping that the national outpouring of grief and outrage caused by the shocking assassination of such a brilliant man would also be dignified. He understood that feelings were riding high but he said that he fully expected all citizens to conduct themselves appropriately and he warned the small minority that might not behave appropriately that they would face immediate and severe actions. The message was clear.

Fr Omar led the funeral service. It was quiet and respectful. It had the definite feeling of the calm before a storm but Fr Omar had made it quite clear to all in the New Cuba movement that today was not the day. Today they would show themselves again but no more. The funeral procession and the small parades in church squares proceeded and again were dignified. Dow, who had pushed hard his hints of outbreaks of civil unrest and clashes with the police even, was disappointed and spent the evening drowning his sorrows in Cuban rum. A clear opportunity had been missed. If it were not for the strong leadership of Fr Omar he would have started to have serious doubts about the potential of the New Cuba movement.

The Russians also had two surprises. In the afternoon the six FSB-secondees were summarily escorted to a military airfield just outside the capital and thanked for their advice which was no longer needed. In the evening the tender for the gold concessions, in which the Russians were rumoured to have already won the two concessions which they wanted, was quietly put on hold as a sign of respect for the assassinated former Minister.

Twenty Eight

FLOXLY had scanned the daily briefing from the British Embassy in Havana. For once it had been informative and it had highlighted the quasi-expulsion of the FSB officers. Floxly was put through to Bunin.

"Vladimir," said Floxly brightly, "how are you?"

"Very good, thank you, David," replied Bunin.

"I notice that your cooperation exercises with the Cubans seem to have been scaled down?" said Floxly with a questioning tone in his voice.

"Oh, just several advisers have returned home, that is all," replied Bunin casually.

"The timing appears a little odd though, Vladimir, when pro-American sentiment seemds to be rising on the island," continued Floxly as if prodding Bunin. "Public demonstrations even rumoured."

"You have very good information as aways, David," replied Bunin his tone reverting to his often brisk if somewhat brusque manner. "But I would not worry too much about American involvement."

"Really?" asked Floxly.

"Yes, if only the CIA could pump enough dirty money into the country then I would be concerned but the banking routes have been closed to such tactics and are heavily monitored. And as you know smuggling is not an option currently. I can understand how frustrating it must feel to the Americans with all their resources and yet not being able to finance a coup in their own backyard."

Floxly could detect the hint of mockery in Bunin's voice and as he was about to reply one of his assistants entered his room and handed him a folder. She mimed that it was 'from President Bunin and for the call they were having'. Floxly nodded his thanks and opened the folder.

"I hope you have received the photographs now, David," continued Bunin after a pause. "I thought that as we are talking about the Americans, you might like to see them."

Floxly studied the photographs. They were of two men on a balcony. One was Kelly. The other man was handing something to Kelly.

"Your Mr Kelly seems to be very much at home in CIA company, David," said Floxly.

"What are they doing?" asked Floxly.

"My sources believe that they are working together. Old style by the looks of it. Exchanging information at the very least," said Bunin who sounded as if he were smiling. "Secret meetings, you know the routine."

Floxly was non-plussed but then why should he be surprised? Recent indications were pointing towards Kelly having deep US links. Information on his uncle was not yet really forthcoming and Cummings had said he suspected a link between Kelly's uncle, who had joined the US Special Forces when he had emigrated, and the US intelligence community in one form or another.

"Anyway, David, back to Cuba. To be on the safe side I am mobilising more of my assets over there especially as your Mr Kelly appears to be up to something with the Americans. Cuba is, after all, a long way from Moscow."

As the call ended Floxly thought long and hard about telling the Americans about Russia upping its efforts in Cuba but then again if Kelly was somehow on the

American side then presumably they should very well know already. Not intervening might also be a way once again to find out who Kelly was working for. He would sit tight.

Twenty Nine

DOW had taken several remedies to counteract his hangover but none seemed to be working. He was in the sacristy with Fr Omar. He had kept a pair of dark sunglasses on when he had sat down at the table.

"You do not look well, my son," said Fr Omar.

"Self-inflicted, Father," replied Dow in a hoarse voice.

"One moment," said Fr Omar as he went to the door of the sacristy and issued a polite request. The sound of scurrying feet then echoed down the inside of the church. Fr Omar returned and sat back down.

"So the funeral went without incident, Father, as you wished," said Dow.

"Yes, it was not the time and the streets were flooded with SDE agents and those who the SDE can so easily bribe to be their spies for the day," replied Fr Omar. He said the word SDE with evident distaste. Dow knew that

Fr Omar had spent some time detained by the SDE when he was a trainee priest in the 1970's and Dow suspected that Fr Omar had endured some nasty treatment but Dow had not wanted to ask about the details. "People are ready to join with us but only if we can provide cash or other resources. Can you tell me now about your plans for this?"

As Fr Omar finished his sentence the door to the sacristy opened and a small boy ran in, put a small purple glass bottle on the table and ran back out again. Fr Omar made the sign of the cross over the boy as he ran out.

"Please drink it," said Fr Omar, "it will help."

Dow picked up the bottle and smelt it. It smelt sweet. He took a large sip and as Fr Omar nodded at him he drank the contents in three gulps. His throat burned and his eyes stung. For a moment Dow felt more intoxicated than he had ever felt before in his entire life and then his body seemed to kick itself all over and then stop.

"Wow," whispered Dow. "What was in that?"

"It is a local potion, John. An ancient recipe from Africa. It used to be used to cure very sick children but we have found that it is a good kick-start to the body after there have been substance abuses."

"Well, it certainly disabused my body!" laughed Dow, "and my brain! Is it a voodoo potion?"

"It is part of Santeria as we call our ancient beliefs," replied Fr Omar with as smile. "Voodoo is the name given to it for tourists."

"And can you believe in it when you are a Catholic priest?" asked Dow.

Fr Omar just smiled and nodded to Dow. "Your plans?" asked Fr Omar again.

This time Dow talked and talked. His tongue had been loosened. It was clear to everyone back home that they could not wire in cash or smuggle in dollar bills as they had originally planned. The Russians would catch them and have damning proof. No, they had started a black op to beat all black ops. They were close to materialising an asset on the island of tremendous value and an asset which was as untraceable as anything on the planet, let alone on the island. Fr Omar encouraged him to talk.

"The asset can be spread all over the island in a couple of days, Father. Everyone will rise with us secure that they have real funds in their own hands and financial security like never before. We just need to confirm the location of the asset. We acquired a copy of a map. It is an ancient map and was a copy drawn by hand. It is very faded and may have errors. We just need to check the original." Dow paused and then continued in a whisper. "The original which a wealthy Spanish family has recently brought back to the island from Spain. Once we can check, we will know."

Thirty

"ANNA, time for a short trip," said Nazarov as he opened the back passenger seat of a purple Chevrolet. Varonsky was driving and Nazarov got back in the front passenger seat.

"Anywhere nice?" asked Anna reverting to her dizzy woman act.

Varonsky grunted but Nazarov replied smoothly. "We are searching for the final piece in a puzzle. A map which will show us a location."

"I thought you had chosen which gold concessions to bid for already," said Anna.

Varonsky grunted again but Nazarov looked at Anna with a grin. "It is never too late to change our mind," he said. "Especially if we can find better information."

Anna did not question any further. She knew from her eavesdropping that they were searching for hidden gold but she wanted to make sure that she did not give away the fact that she knew about the pair's real objective. Varonsky had called her an hour ealier and told her to be ready to be picked up outside her hotel. The car drove through centre of Havana and then to the outskirts and into the Miramar district. It stopped outside a row of villas. The villas were on a beachfront. At the moment there were no signs of anyone but the various household objects lying around the villas indicated that they were all occupied and most likely rented by ex-pat families. Varonsky pointed to the villa at the end and Nazarov motioned for Anna to follow him out of the car. They walked up to the front door of the villa.

"We are enquiring about renting a property," said Nazarov under his breath as he rang the doorbell. Anna understood that she was the cover. She gave a brief shrug of her shoulders.

Nazarov rang again and waited. No one came. As he rang for the third time he put his hands on the lock of the door and in a flash had broken the front door open. Anna stared at him. With a smile Nazarov put a finger to his lips and stepped in. He then had to grab hold of Anna's arm to drag her in and close the door behind them. Anna continued to feign shock and her eyes widened further as she surveyed the room. They were in a large open-plan living and dining room. There was a desk in one corner and police tape around most of the furniture. It was a crime scene and showed the signs of having been thoroughly searched.

"What happened?" said Anna her voice shaky.

"Nothing to worry about," replied Nazarov, "and we are only here to find a map not to steal anything. Now you go upstairs and search the bedrooms. Use your female instincts to see where a man might hide a map or a book which he does not want anyone to find."

Anna did as instructed. She was, of course, extensively trained in the concealment and the uncovering of objects. She had covered the main bedroom, a guest bedroom and two bathrooms in minutes. She found no maps or papers and the only thing she established was that a man lived there whose clothes seemed to be British brands. Having finished she moved quietly to the top of the stairs and looked down below.

Nazarov had found a pile of papers and he was looking through them on a large dining table. Anna raised her eyebrow as she noticed that Nazarov had put a silencer on his Glock which was also on the table. Nazarov had found what looked like a map and he was studying it intensely. He seemed to be really concentrating. His concentration was such that he had not seen a police officer enter the house from a patio door at the back. The police officer had drawn a pistol and was taking a phone from his pocket. The police officer was walking very slowly and as quietly as possible. He was now only a few yards from Nazarov who was still engrossed in studying something. The police officer's pistol was trained on Nazarov.

Anna looked at her handbag. If she shot the noise would be obvious to anyone outside and it would probably echo up and down the beachfront. She took a split second decision and took off one of her shoes. It had a solid heal. She took a step down the stairs.

"Darling," she said loudly, "do you always have to work so hard?"

The surprise of her loud voice distracted the police officer who stopped and automatically pointed his pistol at Anna. Nazarov jumped round as the police officer looked from Anna to Nazarov and back again. Anna siezed the moment and hurled her shoe at the police officer. The police officer was so surprised that he stood still as the heal of the shoe hit him full in the face and he dropped his pistol. In the second that followed Anna lept down the stairs and grabbed the police officer's pistol just as Nazarov picked up and fired his gun and put three bullets into the officer who hit the floor in an instant. Anna also seized the police officer's phone and slickly switched it off.

"My, my," said Nazarov, "and where did you learn that?"

"Self-defence class," said Anna as Nazarov took the police officer's pistol off her. "But I never thought I would have to use it."

"Well, I think we had better offer you a job. Maybe I should talk to my boss?"

The atmosphere was suddenly tense. Nazarov was staring at Anna. He was debating how much to challenge her.

"Is that the President himself?" she asked remembering his previous remarks.

"No, we don't work for him. Our boss has much more power. But let us have this conversation somewhere else and do not tell Varonsky what just happened."

Anna shrugged her shoulders.

"We need to leave," continued Nazarov taking one piece of paper from the table. "Our last stop will have to be his office, after all," he said under his breath. His annoyance at not finding what he wanted was audible.

Anna ignored what he said but made a mental note to warn Kelly as soon as she could. She was sure now that the villa was rented by the dead British geologist and by 'his office' Nazaronv meant the UK company's office. If she and Nazarov were going to run into Kelly, she had better warn him somehow.

Thirty One

IN his hotel room Kelly watched the news with interest. CNN was reporting on Cuba. Two items jolted Kelly. The first was the disappearance of a senior priest in Havana. A Fr Omar had not turned up to celebrate mass in his parish the day before. The priest it was revealed had recently led the funeral service of the assassinated former Minister Xavier de la Rosa and was universally liked in his parish. None of the priest's belongings had been taken and no one had been able to contact the priest now for over twenty-four hours. The most likely explanation seemed to be that he had not left of his own free will and there were growing calls for the police to investigate. Rumours were spreading by word-of-mouth of a return to the dark days of state-sponsored kidnappings by the SDE.

The second item was a surprise but as Kelly listened he could easily understand why. Newgold had announced that following the murder of its geologist and the delay in the tender for the six gold concessions that it was considering merging its Cuban operations with the Canadian company CCMC. Kelly was now convinced that the murder of the geologist was part of a much wider series of events. He thought it time to contact base. He sent a simple text to the switchboard at Number 10. An hour later he had had a message delivered to his room asking him to come to the hotel's business centre. Once again he was shown in to the small booth-type room and picked up the phone.

"Jack," said Floxly, "what's on your mind?"

"There have been other events which may complicate what I have been looking for," replied Kelly. He hoped this oblique-speak would be understood by Floxly.

"Oh, I would not worry," continued Floxly.

"Yes, there was a strange taxi ride which our employee took," said Kelly trying to think of how to explain, "and other similar events."

"I understand," said Floxly, "but I think the case is best closed."

Kelly looked at the phone. He had not expected this.

"And I am glad to say that a large insurance payment has been made to the family. The family is very grateful for all your work. Your return flight has been booked and the hotel will deliver the ticket to you soon. Thank you again." And with that the phone call ended.

Floxly smiled to himself. He had not given Kelly any time to comment or object. He would continue to sit tight and see how Kelly reacted.

Kelly left the room not knowing what to think. He walked into reception and picked up one of the local newspapers. He was stumped good and proper. He went to the hotel bar and ordered a coffee. As the bartender started to make the coffee he also ordered a double Havana Club rum. He flicked through the newspaper. It was an old habit.

On the third page a photograph stood out. It was of the priest who had disappeared. The priest was standing outside a church. He was posing for the photograph with a small group of women. Kelly looked intently as he sipped his rum. One of the women had a striking resemblence to Maria. Kelly read the title of the article: 'Missing Catholic priest has links to Santeria cult'. The link did not bother Kelly. It was the presence of Maria. He could not leave now.

As he finished his rum a receptionist from the hotel came over to him with an envelope. My ticket home, thought Kelly as he thanked the young woman. He opened it. There was no ticket but a message. The message was a jumble of letters in the cyrillic alphabet in four small blocks with a large 'A' and 'P' at the bottom. This was old-style. He needed to work out the key and then transpose the jumbled up letters. The key was easy. The KGB had always had a bizarre fondness for Russian literature. This was most likely Alexander Pushkin, Russia's most renowned poet. Kelly could still recite several of Pushkin's most famous verses from his student days by heart. Within twenty minutes he had cracked the code. The message read: 'Newgold office be careful'. He now knew where to go but before he did so he dialled a number. He wanted to speak to the Americans.

Thirty Two

DOW'S mobile rang at the most inconvenient time. He was enjoying an athletic siesta with Maria. He glanced at the number but let the phone ring. 'So the Brits need our help!' he thought to himself for a second before being plunged back into Maria's embrace. Ever since Fr Omar had given him the potion in the purple bottle he had been hyperactive and Maria had not needed to give him any encouragement from the moment he had arrived. Maria had prepared herself in her normal way. She had bathed and then put on a black negligee under a red silk dressing gown. She put her hair up and looked a million dollars. Her skin shone and her eyes sparkled. She had also lit several scented candles in her bedroom and also an additional one hidden inside a wardrobe.

Twenty minutes later Dow was on his back with his eyes closed. Maria had watched him slowly fall asleep. She knew he would now sleep for at least an hour. The laced aperitif drink would see to that. She got out of her bed and after taking a small key from her jewellery box she opened a wardrobe. A waft of strong incense filled the room. Her altar was a mini scene out of the underworld. Old pictures of saints and less reputable beings with horns and contorted bodies were stuck to the wall. Potion bottles full of dark liquids were placed around the centrepiece – a small skull similar to a human one but rounder. A stick of incense was protruding from the top of the skull and suspended from a noose was a doll made of bones, twine and dressed in a suit. It was the image of Dow. Maria took hold of the doll and gently poked a small needle into one of its legs. Behind her on the bed Dow's leg buckled. Maria could feel the movement of his body as a vibration passed down the leg of the bed and rippled across the floor to where she was kneeling. She let go of the doll and closed her eyes.

In her mind she reran part of their time in bed and she smiled. She had been so powerful. She had moaned to him that he was her darling, that everything she was doing was for his cause and the cause of a New Cuba. He had believed her every word and no matter what he would see or watch Maria do in the next days, he would believe this to the end. She had him where she wanted him. He would serve.

Maria then took Dow's mobile and dialled the missed call.

"Thanks for calling back," said a happy-sounding Kelly.

"Be careful," whispered Maria disguising her voice completely and hanging up.

Thirty Three

FOLLOWING his second warning Kelly jumped into a taxi and went straight to the Newgold office in the Miramar Trade Centre. It was late morning but there seemed to be no one in. Kelly rang the bell and tried to look through a frosted glass window into the reception area behind the door. No movement. The building had a concierge on the ground floor, a fairly old woman whom Kelly had seen when he had been to the office previously. Five minutes later and having donated an incentive to the woman Kelly was let in by her 'to pick up some papers he needed before flying back to England'.

Kelly found the dead geologist's desk in an instant. It was covered in papers and the working tools of a geologist. The desk was a simple construction of a top and four legs with a set of drawers on the right. Kelly was sweating and he was becoming nervous. He took a deep breath and then started on the desk. He had been well trained in searching. He ignored the papers and instruments on the desk and instead made a mental image of the desk and drawers in his head. If the information, the map or a set of coordinates was that important then whatever it was would be concealed with deliberate care. In his mind he then lifted up a three-dimension model of the desk and its drawers and turned it upside down. He then looked back at the desk and ducked down. He felt under the top of the desk. Nothing. He then pulled out the top drawer and felt underneath the bottom of the drawer. Nothing. He did the same for the remaining two drawers and there it was. A piece of paper in a plastic wallet stuck under the bottom of the last drawer!

He took the piece of paper out of the plastic wallet and unfolded it. It was a map of Western Cuba with notes and circles drawn by hand. He looked at other papers on the desk and the handwriting matched that of the dead geologist. Raven had been right when he said that the geologist's work had been left in the office but would anyone have expected this? The geologist was either paranoid about sharing his work with his colleagues or he was working to his own agenda. There was also the further possibility that he was working under someone else's orders. Kelly heard a noise and froze.

Outside the purple Chevrolet had driven up and had parked across from the office building. Anna was again sitting in the back with Nazarov and Varonsky in the front. As Anna opened her door Nazarov turned round.

"You stay outside this time," said Nazarov. "We will be on the fifth floor of this building. Stand by the main door and if anyone comes into the building you need to warn us."

"How will I do that?" asked Anna.

"I am sure you will find a way," replied Nazarov with a smirk.

Anna did as she was instructed but not without a wave of panic. She wanted to warn Kelly and hoped that he had not yet come to the office. She composed herself and after a couple of minutes she walked back to the car. She opened the driver's door and looked in. She placed a small mobile phone under the seat jamming it out of sight. She had switched it on and put it on silent. She could now track the phone's location and with it the Chevrolet.

Thirty Four

DOW had never felt so elated and it was made more so by the sight of the man being pushed down the side of the church in a wheelchair. Gifford. One minute Dow was enjoying the wife and next the husband had come to beg. To beg for a way home. Dow would enjoy the next few moments. He went back into the sacristy. He had placed a folder on the table.

"Is he coming?" asked Fr Omar. Fr Omar was dressed in civilian clothes.

"Yes," replied Dow, "and you can set off as soon as you wish, Father. There is a van outside and you can hide in the back when needed."

Fr Omar nodded. Dow had wanted to have Gifford on his own but Fr Omar looked as though he was staying. Fr Omar was about to leave and set off on a clandestine tour of key parishes in Havana and targetted other cities and towns. His job was to spread the word of the coming of the New Cuba, to inspire the uprising, to guarantee that the funds would be arriving. Funds to give so many families a real rise in their standard of living, the true basis for a nation freed from dictatorship and a true mark of faith from the free world and given, of course, with such generosity by their cousins across the Florida Straits.

"If I know for sure that the asset can be found I will take much confidence with me," said Fr Omar with a smile as the door to the sacristy was opened and the wheelchair was pushed in.

"Father Omar," began a flustered Gifford, "we thought you were missing."

"Only for a short while, Gifford," replied Fr Omar. "A delicate assignment. How are you feeling?"

"The pain in my neck spread to my back and I can't really walk. That is why I have to fly back to England at once and I need money for treatment in a private hospital."

"Of course," said Dow putting two bundles on the table. "I have ten thousand as agreed."

"And I can give you this," replied Gifford handing Dow two folded sheets of paper.

"Father, can you assist Gifford to leave while I check this?"

Fr Omar nodded and took hold of the wheelchair. Dow opened the folder he had put on the table when he had arrived and took out two old maps. The original was stunning. La Carta del Oro Osculto. The map which had been in the de la Pena family for centuries and which he had courted its owner so ardently to win it from her. He had made her think that her dream of finding her familiy's vast lost wealth would come true with his help. He picked up the copy which had been acquired in Miami. There were two mistakes in the copy and mistakes big enough to render the copy inaccurate.

Dow then unfolded the two pieces of paper Gifford had provided. They were photocopies of a modern day map. So that is how Gifford said he had gotten hold of the dead geologist's last workings. Gifford had photocopied well. Dow lay the original map and then the photocopies of the modern map side by side. In an instant he had the spot. It was right on the coast north of Pinar del Rio. It was one hundred and twenty miles from Havana which by road could take anything from four to five hours by car. He had another plan.

As Fr Omar peered around the door Dow turned round and nodded. He made the sign of 'ok' with the fingers of one hand and put a finger from his other hand

to his lips. Nothing more would be said. The green light
was on.

Thirty Five

KELLY had tucked the plastic folder in his belt at the back of his trousers and listened. Footsteps. Very careful footsteps. And then a smash. As Kelly looked around the office for another way out, the two men burst into the office and Kelly could sense the telltale feeling of guns being trained on him. He was helpless.

"I thought your office was closing down," said Nazarov in good English. "That is, if this is actually your office?"

A flash of panic shot across Kelly's face as the second man moved behind him. Instinctively Kelly had raised his arms. In Russian Varonsky asked if he should shoot Kelly. Kelly did well not to react. He just looked surprised at hearing foreign words.

"Not yet," continued Nazarov in English, "and if he gives us what we came for we may not need to shoot him."

Kelly spoke with a large gulp. "What do you mean?" he said. "I am just a consultant to the company. What have you come for?"

"A map," replied Nazarov. "A map drawn by your geologist."

"This is his desk," said Kelly stepping forward and pointing to the desk. Reacting to his movement Varonsky grabbed Kelly's arm from behind and pulled him down. As he was forced down the folder flipped out of his belt.

"Excellent work, Pavel. Your rough tactics have worked at last," said Nazarov picking up the folder. "The latest map, I presume."

Kelly got to his feet. He was sorely tempted to attack the man who had grabbed him but as each of them had a gun he decided he would have to wait for a better chance.

"Now, I was going to let you go," continued Nazarov, "but you seem to also want to have this map, so that will not be possible. But it might not be a good idea to shoot you here. That too would create unwelcome attention. Come with us."

Nazarov and Varonsky hastily hid their guns as they pushed Kelly out of the entrance to the building and onto the street. They stepped over to the car. Anna could not hide her surprise as she saw them with another person with them but the fact that she was surprised did not concern Nazarov who told Anna to get in the front passenger seat and Kelly to get into the back. Nazarov then sat next to Kelly and took out his gun again.

"I have a final job for you," Nazarov said to Anna. "We will drop you and our new guest in a special place and then come and get you tomorrow."

Varonsky laughed at the words 'special place' and Anna glared at him. She would do as instructed but only to a point. Nazarov looked as though he had what he wanted and she presumed that he and Varonsky would now go and find the doubloons she had overheard them discussing. She hoped that she would soon be on their trail.

The 'special place' announced itself in black letters above a door to a cellar. They had driven into a compound which had steel gates. Varonsky had had a key. They got out of the car and Varonsky pushed the cellar door open. Kelly approached the door first and read the black letters. They were in Spanish: 'Bienvenidos a la casa muetra'.

"Welcome to the dead house," said Kelly.

"Oh, they are alive. Well, some of them, sort of," laughed Nazarov as he pushed Kelly and then Anna through the door. "They will take good care of you," he said as he closed the door after them.

Anna grabbed Kelly's hand as their eyes adjusted to the darkness.

"Jack," she whispered. "Did you get my message?"

"Yes," replied Kelly. "I went there straight away and was just about to leave. I guess they are from Cyprus Gold and they are hunting for the ancient gold rather than the concessions and something tells me that they are not the only ones looking for it."

"Once we get out of here, I'll be able to follow them," replied Anna who then screamed. In front of them swayed three men. There faces were deathly pale. Their eyes were closed, their bodies stank. And then a beep of a horn. The flash of a headlight. They both knew what was coming. A whoosh in the air and the smashing of glass into pieces. Screeching tyres and gunshots. The zoombies had come out to play. A whip cracked followed by silence. A petrifying silence.

Thirty Six

AS Anna increased her grip on Kelly, a pair of hands grabbed Kelly from behind and a cool breath of fresh air swirled around them as did an increasing pool of light. Kelly did not hesitate. He turned round grabbing Anna and they shot out of the door to the cellar which the pair of hands had opened for them. Kelly slammed the door shut and look around him. The sight made him go weak at the knees. Her beauty had increased. Her face was younger, her hair darker and longer. Her black dress accentuated her curves. Her eyes were on fire.

"Are you not going to introduce me, Jack?" said Maria in a such a sultry Spanish accent that Jack's throat went dry.

"Maria Thellwall-Jones, this is Pulkova, Anastasia Ivanovna," said Jack his voice rising. He remembered Anna's real name which he thought it better to use.

"Anna is better, though," said Anna.

"And such a Russian beauty," said Maria with a large smile. "My, my, Jack and how do you know each other? She would have been a schoolgirl when you were in Moscow."

Anna looked in puzzlement at Kelly.

"We have worked together recently," replied Jack. "And actually now that I think back it was your father and your sister perhaps who I met in Moscow, was it not, Maria?"

"It was," said Maria with another smile, "and we have forgiven you for choosing the American company over us. Our purpose in going to Russia was to find the copy of our map. We knew that several copies had been made for a Dutch explorer who was actually more of a pirate and who had had them made secretly. The one in the Hermitage had been sold to someone in Peter the Great's entourage no doubt with a tale of lost treasure to match. Another copy we knew had made its way to somewhere in the States, again a dubious sale no doubt to an unsuspecting treasure hunter."

"How did you know that we were here?" asked Kelly, the mystery of the maps now finally clear.

"Jack, with all your training surely you have worked that out," replied Maria who picked up a large red silk gown which was on the floor near her feet and swirled it around her. She was immediately transformed. Anna had taken out her handgun from her bag. "But maybe not," continued Maria as she pulled the hood of the gown over her head. Her body emanated magic, black magic.

"Are you a witch?" said Anna. There was meance in her voice and she had raised her handgun.

"A priestess," replied Maria. "And a priestess who has been looking after you."

"Looking after?" asked Jack his voice rising.

"Ever since you have been on the island my, how do you say? - my 'religious' friends - have been watching and playing with you both. Just think of the faces."

Kelly's mind kicked into overdrive as it recalled all the pale faces, lifeless eyes and slow moving people he had seen virtually everywhere he had been.

"Jack, I have released you," said Maria grabbing hold of Kelly's arm. "And now you must do me one favour in return. I know you found the new map which the geologist was finalising. I just need the place. You see an earthquake in 1789 radically changed the area along the Western coast. The chests had been hidden in an old disused mine which still had some deep deposits of gold but they were impossible to mine in the old days. There was access to the mine via caves at the bottom of the cliffs as well as through the mineshaft but the earthquake sent part of the cliffs into the sea. Your geologist was working in the area and using some very sophisticated equipment. We are sure he found the old mine."

Jack closed his eyes and recited a short burst of numbers and letters. They were map coordinates and both women memorised them instantly. Once more Jack was thankful for the hours and hours of memory training he had had to endure to create a quasi-photographic memory. The moment he had found the map in the folder under the drawer he had scanned the map in a flash and with a simple close of his eyes he could see it again as if it were right infront of him.

Maria was gone before Anna and Kelly could stop her. She had left her red silk gown and Kelly bent down to pick it up. As he did so the gown rose, billowing up. Kelly grabbed it and jumped back in horror. A face. A dead face. Female. Its mouth open, its eyes missing. It screamed at him. A scream from hell. Then the gown flopped back on the ground. He knew he would see her face again. It was a message – a message from the future.

Thirty Seven

ANNA had been able to track the Chevrolet on her mobile as Kelly drove a Suzuki Jeep they had rented from their hotel. They had driven along the A4 from Havana to Pinar del Rio and then turned up to the coast on towards a small town called Santa Lucia. They had a good map and navigated relatively easily. The vegetation at either side of the roads was thick and they were both intrigued by the prevalence of a special type of geological formation, a type of hill called a mogote, a steep-sided hill with a rounded tower-like top. The car hire assistant had explained to them in great detail that these mogotes were unique to Cuba.

They drove straight through Santa Lucia and then turned onto a track heading for the nearby coast. As they started down the track they noticed that a purple Chevrolet had stopped about a mile further on. Anna was sure that it was Nazarov and Varonsky's car. They drove down the track slowly and a couple of hundered yards from the Chevrolet they reversed off the track so that the Jeep was out of sight.

As they got out of the Jeep they heard a helicopter overhead. Kelly looked up and caught a glimpse of the helicopter. He had expected a Cuban or Russian military helicopter as they were almost at the coast where some of the cooperation exercises were being carried out. The helicopter was very modern looking and very black. It had to be American related.

The area ahead of them did not ressemble that of an old mine. Kelly and Anna jogged down the track. The track was well used and either side were tall palm and pine trees and plants some of which Kelly recognised as tobacco plants. As they turned a bend they saw a tall outcrop of land in front of them and as they both stopped to survey the area they could hear waves breaking onto a shore in the distance. Other than a small thatched building with boarded-up windows and some rusting iron machinery parts there did not seem to be anything else.

Kelly studied the outcrop. It looked like a mogote, one of the odd hills they had seen en route, but as he looked intensely at the rocks overgrown with trees and bushes something struck him. The edge of the outcrop was sheer and not rounded as most of the mogotes were.

Maria had been right. There must have been an earthquake here which had taken a chunk of the cliff into the sea or the ground. He could also see some dark coloured objects which did not appear to be natural vegetation and then a movement. Several quick movements near the top of the rock. Again the movements were not those of a natural being, of an animal. Someone was up there. The area Kelly could now see was a small plateau-like clearing.

As Kelly pointed up to the area to Anna two shots rang out ahead of them and the peacefulness of the area was shattered. Anna and Kelly both ducked down instinctively and Anna had her handgun in her hand in an instant. A figure ran out from the area up at the top of the rock and started to fire. It was a man and he was making his way around the cliff away from the opening he had come out. Another shot and Anna tugged on Kelly's sleeve.

"Over there," she whispered, "I just saw Varonsky. I think they must be heading up the rock as well."

"Cover me, Anna," said Kelly, "I need to get inside the cliff."

Kelly did not give Anna time to object as he rushed off. The man with two others now about a hundred yards behind him were heading out of view. Anna followed Kelly. To Kelly's surprise and relief as he reached the bottom of the rock he saw a narrow winding path going up. With a series of quick jumps and steps he reached the spot where the man had come out. The small clearing was well disguised by the bushes and trees. There was a rusted narrow-guage rail track which went into the cliff. Kelly examined the track and whistled as he followed it from the opening in the cliff to the edge of the cliff where it stopped. It overhang the edge by a couple of feet. The rest of the track and the cliff were missing. Obvious earthquake damage, thought Kelly. He looked at the end of the track which was twisted where it had been sheered off. Down below about a hundred feet was the sea.

As another burst of gunfire sounded from the other side of the cliff Kelly jumped up and made his way to the opening. The opening was an entrance to a mineshaft. Kelly peered in and listened. Silence. He waited a few seconds as his eyes adjusted to the darkness. The darkness was not total. There were several shafts of light ahead. Probably from air tunnels, thought Kelly. Ahead of him he saw two tunnels both sloping downwards. The narrow gauage track split into two just inside the entrance and went down both tunnels. Which tunnel? Left or right?

He looked at the roofs of the tunnels and then stepped forward into the tunnel on the right. He lifted his foot to take the next step. A sound of pain. He looked up. A face was hovering, suspended in mid-air. A dead face. The face of the screamimg woman, mouth open, her eyes this time burning red. Kelly slowly pulled back his foot and stepped back ever so carefully. He closed his eyes and the dead woman's face vanished with a cry. A cry this time not of pain but of farewell. The message had been delivered.

Kelly peered down the tunnel he had stepped back from. A streak of light came from the roof above and Kelly began to make out a shape below. The tunnel had dropped sharply and had he stepped forward he would have fallen down. Several yards below lay a body facedown. Its head was at an angle to its body. A stake was protruding through its back and Kelly could now make out a gun holster under a jacket. He was pretty sure it was CIA-issue but the body was not that of Dow. The ancient gold had claimed another victim and it must have been Dow who he had seen exit the mineshaft. Kelly heard several dull but strong sounds. Gunshots. Dow must be fighting with the Russians.

Kelly now speeded up and moved into the tunnel on the left. Dow had been very busy before being disturbed. Two trucks were on the track just inside the entrance and both of them were loaded full of old wooden chests. As Kelly stepped forward, a figure slowly and silently moved deeper into the shadows in the tunnel. Quickly Kelly opened the first chest. A golden dust swirled upwards and Kelly was back in the harsh winter in Moscow. Piles and piles of ancient gold coins. If each chest contained as much as this one, then there were thousands and thousands. The value Anna had told him she had calculated looked eminently possible. And what a way to finance an operation, he whistled to himself, finally realising exactly what was being planned.

It took all Kelly's strength to pull the two trucks along the track out of the opening. The effort was immense and after he had pushed them into the small clearing he bent over, put his hands on his knees and took a deep breath. A figure also emerged silently from the mineshaft entrance and hid behind a vine to the side of the entrance. Kelly looked down the path and could see Anna positioned halfway up with her handgun drawn clearly expecting the others to appear at any moment.

Kelly opened the chest on top once again. It was time to think. If the Americans took the gold then regime change in Cuba would be financed at a stroke. Each doubloon had an immense value and they were the perfect size to distribute across the whole of the island and in no time at all. He could just imagine the effect one doubloon would have on a family's living standard. On the other hand, if the rogue Russian agents took the chests, then Cuba would stay under Russian influence and would it matter that the FSB agents had defied Bunin? Although this was something which Anna seemed to be extremely concerned about and which Kelly could understand. No one defied Bunin for long.

Kelly's analysis was cut short by a laugh. Dow, his hands tied behind his back and with a deep gash across his forehead was pushed into the small clearing followed by Narazov and Varonsky. They both stared at the two trucks and wooden chests and tucked their guns in the back of their trousers. Varonsky pushed Dow to the ground.

"So you escaped the zoombies. That is a surprise. And you have even been so kind as to bring the gold out for us," said Nazarov with a large smile.

Kelly realised that he was standing there unarmed. He looked around for anything he could use to defend himself.

"I guess that it is also the end of the planned American coup, as well," said Nazarov as he looked down at Dow. "So close, my friend. Langley would have been so, so proud. A gold coup by a golden agent."

As Nazarov and Varonsky were about to move towards the trucks, a figure rushed out of the vine and jumped in front of Kelly. It was clothed in a black gown with a hood and pointed an object at Nazarov and Varonsky which it held in front but which was covered by the gown's long sleeve.

"Stop!" screamed a woman's voice. "The coup is happening. No one can stop it. John, carino, get up."

"Maria," shouted Kelly, "are you CIA as well?" Kelly sounded truely shocked.

"And you think your black magic can stop us," sneered Nazarov staring at the stick-like object under the cloak.

"Si," shouted Maria uncovering her head and then throwing off her gown. Narazov and Varonsky looked startled and as Maria pointed a Smith and Weston automatic pistol at them, Kelly acted. With Maria infront of him and facing Nazarov and Varonsky he pushed the second truck with all his might. The gradient to the edge of the cliff was ever so slight but it was downwards. Horror scorched across all the faces. The trucks were moving. Varonsky and Nazarov jumped in front of them and started to push them back whilst Maria tried to pulled the second one back.

The next ten seconds were all in slow motion. The faces of Nazarov and Varonsky bulged as their blood vessels popped to the surface of their skin with the superhuman effort they were making to stop the trucks. Maria had grabbed the back of the second truck with a hand at each side and Dow, who had managed to free his hands, was now behind her pulling her back like a human chain. For one second the wheels on the trucks stopped but a screeching sound became louder and louder. The trucks were still moving.

Gravity and the sheer weight of over half a ton of precious metal were winning slowly. Ever so slowly but surely. None of the four dared let go. Their faces were contorting with anger, then fear, then effort again. Anna had reached the clearing and she stood open-mouthed. With shouts of panic and then vollies of obscenities the Russians were first over the edge. Narazow flung himself to the left and frantically grappled to hold a vine. A soft thud resounded below and then with a heavy creak the first truck went over and thousands of tiny peels of sounds filled the air as the first doubloons were tipped out of the chests and clinked against each other before plopping into the water below. A second heavy creak and another chorus of clinking sounds. And then a high-pitched scream of anguish as Maria tried to stop her body's momentum but found herself in the air. Dow tried desperately to reach her but her fingers fell through his and with a final quiet scream her body splashed into the sea.

As Dow turned to face Kelly, Anna drop-kicked him in the chest in a flash and sent him sprawling across the ground back towards the mineshaft entrance.

"Anna," shouted Kelly who was about to object to her action but stopped himself. "Anna," he said looking behind her, "watch out!"

Nazarov had scrambled back over the edge of the cliff and he was getting to his feet behind her. Anna stepped to the side. Nazarov put his hand behind his back but then swore. He had lost his gun. Anna raised her gun.

"Shoot him," commanded Nazarov motioning towards Kelly. "On the orders of Zelinsky, who I know you know only too well, you are ordered to shoot him."

The comment about Anna knowing Zelinsky made her look at Nazarov with a frown.

"You are too obvious, Pulkova, Anastasia Ivanova. Lieutenant Colonel Pulkova to be more precise," said Nazarov using Anna's real name and FSB title. "If you do not believe me, throw me you phone and I will call Zelinsky. Zelinsky is the boss of us both." Nazarov pronounced 'both' with relish.

Anna steadied herself and took one hand off her gun. She took her mobile out of her pocket. "I will call my boss," she said.

Kelly had raised his hands. Images of rogue Russian agents surrounded by piles and piles of gold coins and celebrating like crazy filled his brain. Had everything he had done led to this? He had finally failed. He had failed even more than the CIA!

"Da," said Anna calmly and quietly as she put her phone in her pocket. She held up her gun and without the slightest tremble she pressed the trigger.

Thirty Eight

FLOXLY had smiled watching the CNN report from Cuba. 'Last Stop Havana finally for the Santa Monica's long-lost gold' ran the headline across the screen. Pictures showed a whole armada of boats surrounding an idyllic part of the Western Cuban coast. A minor earthquake was believed to have hit the cliff along the coast near a village called Santa Lucia sending tonnes and tonnes of rocks into the sea and unearthing the hidden chests of gold doubloons in the process. The doubloons had been readily identified as from the reign of Charles II which had been on the Santa Monica on its fateful last journey from Peru to Spain in 1667. The de la Pena family were on a flight from Madrid and a deal was being negotiated between the family and the Cuban authorities on how to split this massive find which was being hailed as one, if not, the biggest treasure finds ever. Russian naval forces had not being invited to assist the Cuban navy whose divers were rapidly gathering up the doubloons from the shallow waters. The mystery of the Carta del Oro Oculto and the Last Stop of the hidden gold was solved once and for all.

"Well, David," said Bunin, "you were right about how serious the Americans were about Cuba." Bunin had called Floxly.

"Yes, I was surprised myself how serious they were in the first place," replied Floxly. "It seemed a huge risk and so unfeasible in this day and age."

"Well, if they had found the gold for themselves, then they would have had an untraceable and major source of funds to distribute to the people on the island. It would have been a real first and they were so close. A coup financed through old Spanish gold would have been so historically symbolic as well," continued Bunin who sounded genuinely impressed by what the Americans had tried to do.

"But now the Cubans themselves and the Spanish family can split the money."

"Such a shame that we forgave so much of their Soviet debts so recently," said Bunin with a smile, "or else I would have insisted on taking a cut!"

Floxly believed that Bunin would not have hesitated to claim his share if he had half a chance.

"Cuba is calm again," continued Bunin, "but I have some rather unsettling news, David."

"How so?" asked Floxly.

"The head of my FSB, Igor Zelinsky, suffered a fatal heart attack during an interrogation in the Lubyanka this morning," said Bunin.

"My condolences," replied Floxly, "I know he was a very old colleague of yours, Vladimir." The mental image of the head of the FSB himself dying as he tortured some poor dissident in the basement of the FSB headquarters flashed through Floxly's mind and he did not know quite whether he should be pleased or not.

"Yes, we went back a long, long way. In fact too far," said Bunin. His voice had become very, very sombre.

Floxly had never heard Bunin speak in such a manner. The mental image in Floxly's brain flicked round one hundred and eighty degrees as the realisation dawned on him of what Bunin was saying had literally been correct. Zelinsky was the one being interrogated.

"Yes," continued Bunin, "such familiarity can blind us to the actions of those closest to us. It was a great shame for him as he had just entered into a very lucrative deal for his retirement in the sunshine. In fact, if he and his helpers had succeeded in their private venture they would have become richer that anyone in the whole of Cuba."

"I see," said Floxly, "they also wanted the ancient gold but for themselves."

"Yes, and very surprisingly your Jack Kelly put regional political stability ahead of American interests which was a bit of what I think you call a 'turn-up for the books' given his US links."

"Kelly's allegiances remain a mystery," replied Floxly. Floxly had been given a potted summary by his Ambassador in Havana of what had happened at the disused mine and how the doubloons had been pushed over the cliff but he did not have a detailed account and he had resigned himself to never having one. Kelly's US links were still being investigated.

"Do I understand correctly that your female agent disobeyed a direct order at the end, Vladimir?" then asked Floxly. He was keen to win a point off Bunin for once.

"Better to say that I left it to her to use her initiative and she is a very bright young woman," replied Bunin with a smile and ending the call.

Thirty Nine

ANNA had insisted on pushing the injured Dow into the entrance to the mineshaft, gagging him and tying him up so that he could not get out or attract any attention especially if the helicopter started to look for him. She promised Kelly that she would have a message sent to Langley once they were out of the area. This was probably just as well because as they arrived back on the track and were making their way to where they had hidden the Jeep they saw a convoy of vehicles blocking the track. A group of local-looking men were standing around the vehicles. Kelly spotted several shotguns and a number of machetes.

"Who do you think they are, Jack?" asked Anna quietly.

"My guess would be that they are expecting Dow," said Kelly, "and the gold."

Kelly walked straight towards the convoy. The men began to look at Kelly menacingly and voices started to rise. Anna stayed behind Kelly. Her gun was in her bag on her shoulder. As Kelly came close, the group parted and a man dressed in black came through.

"May I help you?" asked the man.

"Father?" replied Kelly recognising the priest from the photographs on the TV and in the newspapers. "Father Omar?" he asked.

"Yes," replied Fr Omar. "And you must be the Englishman Maria spoke of."

"Kelly. Jack Kelly," said Kelly extending his hand.

"Can I offer you a lift?" asked Fr Omar. "The roads may not be safe."

Kelly thought for a moment. "Thank you, Father, but we have transport." Kelly was now standing close to Fr Omar. Kelly put his hand in his pocket and carefully pulled out a handful of gold coins which he gave to Fr Omar. "The rest are in the sea, Father," continued Kelly carefully under his breath. "There was no other choice."

Fr Omar fixed Kelly with a firm look. Kelly could sense a deep sadness overcome the priest. "You may go, my son," he said gravely after a moment. "And may God be with you."

In the Jeep there was an initial silence until they were far enough away from the convoy. Kelly put his hand into his other pocket and pulled out another handful of gold coins which he gave to Anna.

"Jack," said Anna, "I thought back there that they were going to take us prisoner then but it seems that you have friends in the strangest places."

"And possibly in the Kremlin even?" asked Kelly. Anna had shot Nazarov in ice-cold blood. Kelly presumed that she had acted on the order of Bunin.

"Oh, no!" replied Anna with a wide smile and a toss of her blond hair. "He said it was for me to choose!"

"Well, that calls for a celebration, Anna!" said Kelly who did not know quite how to react. "One last stop, then, in Havana?"

"What do you have in mind?" asked Anna.

"Oh, there are one or two places which I would like to visit again and hopefully banish a few ghosts," said Kelly with a smile.

"Jack, are you completely mad?" laughed Anna. "I am never going to any of those places again in my life."

"Some salsa music then?" asked Kelly smiling again. "And just one last drink, perhaps?"

"Just one last drink," sighed Anna, "and it will definitely be the last stop in Havana, Jack. The last stop this time for sure."